WS

THE CINNAMON TREE

'Aubrey Flegg, who recently won the Peter Pan
Prize 2000 for his first book, *Katie's War*, has again
come up with a very likeable heroine in
The Cinnamon Tree'
Margrit Cruickshank, The Irish Times

AUBREY FLEGG was born in Dublin. His early childhood was spent in County Sligo, Ireland. He went to school in Dublin and later in England. After a spell with a mountain rescue team in Scotland, he returned to Ireland to study geology at Trinity College. He then did geological research in Kenya, before joining the Geological Survey of Ireland in 1968. His first book, *Katie's War,* is about the civil war period in Ireland; it was published in 1997. *Katie's War* won the Peter Pan Award 2000 – an award created by IBBY Sweden for a children's book, translated into Swedish, which gives information on another culture. *Katie's War* is currently being translated into German.

Aubrey recently took early retirement in order to concentrate on writing. He has had one short story for adults published. This is his second novel for children.

The CINNAMON TREE

AUBREY FLEGG

THE O'BRIEN PRESS
DUBLIN

First published 2000 by The O'Brien Press Ltd.,
20 Victoria Road, Dublin 6, Ireland.
Tel. +353 1 4923333; Fax. +353 1 4922777
E-mail books@obrien.ie
Website www.obrien.ie
Reprinted 2000

ISBN:0-86278-657-6

British Library Cataloguing-in-Publication Data
Flegg, A.M.
The cinnamon tree : a novel set in Africa
1.Land mines - Africa - Juvenile fiction 2.Children's stories
I.Title
823.9'14[J]

2 3 4 5 6 7 8 9 10
00 01 02 03 04 05 06 07

The O'Brien Press receives
assistance from

The Arts Council
An Chomhairle Ealaíon

Editing, typesetting, layout, design: The O'Brien Press Ltd.
Front cover, background image: courtesy Christaan Clotworthy.
Colour separations: C&A Print Services Ltd.
Printing: Guernsey Press Ltd.

DISCLAIMER

This book is a work of fiction. Characters, incidents and
names have no connection with any country, organisation
or persons alive or dead. Any apparent resemblance is
purely coincidental.

DEDICATION

To Vincent,
friend and representative
of all the local people around the world who go
out every day and risk their lives to make their
countries safe from landmines.

ACKNOWLEDGEMENTS

This book could not have been achieved without the assistance of a number of organisations, and an even greater number of individuals (many now friends). Most significant has been the support and encouragement I received from *Norwegian People's Aid,* who not only allowed me to visit their demining operations in Angola, but also looked after me for the duration of my visit there.

I also want to thank my former trade union, *IMPACT,* for their contribution to my travel expenses.

Individually I want to thank *Niamh O'Rourke,* herself a veteran of landmine rehabilitation in Cambodia, who sparked my interest and introduced me to *Tony D'Costa,* of *Pax Christi Ireland.* Tony is one of the architects of the enormously successful Campaign to Ban Landmines. It was through Tony that I was introduced to Norwegian People's Aid. Here my thanks go to *Per Nergaard,* in Oslo, who organised my visit to Angola, and also to *Håvard Bach,* the NPA Programme Manager in the capital, Luanda, who planned my stay. *Dr Guy Rhodes,* Programme Manager in Lobito ensured that I saw all relevant aspects of the demining operations: manual, mechanical and even the training of dogs. Through Håvard and Guy, I would like to thank all the staff, Angolan and European, who looked after me in Angola, mentioning in particular *Hans Kampenhøy,* and *Vincent* (Adriano Vincente Augusto), to whom this book is dedicated.

In Dublin I was made welcome at two key rehabilitation centres. At the *Central Remedial Clinic* my thanks to fellow author *Jane Mitchell* and to *Joan Hurley*. At the *National Medical Rehabilitation Centre, Charles Murray* and *Michael Sweeney* showed me how artificial legs are prepared for individual patients.

For advice on child soldiers I must thank *Dr James O'Connell* of the *Department of Peace Studies, Bradford, England*, for introducing me to *Dr Ananda Millard* of that department. Ananda's help was invaluable, both for her wide knowledge and her generosity in allowing me to read transcripts of her live interviews with child soldiers. *Mike Bourne* helped me with essential information on the arms trade. Back at home, *Joe Murray* of *Afri* gave me valuable information on the arms trade in Ireland.

My thanks to all of these people. Any inaccuracies or biases that may have crept in are entirely of my own making.

Heartfelt thanks to my wife, Jennifer, for her support throughout – even when I said that I wanted to visit a minefield in Africa. And finally my thanks to my editors, Íde ní Laoghaire and Rachel Pierce, and to all the staff at The O'Brien Press who have worked so hard and enthusiastically to make this book. My final thanks to Aoife Webb, whose inspired comments were such a help in the final stages of this book.

CONTENTS

PROLOGUE

I want to be back in Africa. I want to look up at the night sky and feel the earth spinning beneath me while the stars hunt above. She told me you could hear star voices if you listened really hard. I heard nothing but the soft sound of her breathing as she stood beside me, as invisible as Africa in the night.

Diary of Fintan O'Farrell.

1

The Cinnamon Tree

'Yola ... Yola ...'

The girl stopped her grinding for a moment. On the stone slab in front of her the white maize flour gleamed. She listened ... nothing. She leant forward and swept the hard, yellow, unground maize into the path of her grindstone. She hated this job; it was tiring and cramping for legs that longed to run. The stone rumbled over the hard grains. Then she heard the voice again.

'Yola ... Managu has gone away!'

The treble voice of Gabbin, her little cousin, sounded frightened. Managu was the herd's bull, and Father's pride and joy. Managu was a magnificent bull with huge spreading horns, the leader of the whole herd. If Managu were hurt, poor Gabbin would get the beating of his life and a shame that would last forever. How could Gabbin lose the bull? He was nine years old, too young to be left in charge of the whole herd anyway; if Yola were allowed she would herd the cattle like a boy – she'd take a book with her and read, you could do nothing while grinding.

She turned a basket upside down over the ground maize to keep away the hens and stood for a moment as pins and needles chased through her legs. She was fond of Gabbin. He was her first cousin and an orphan from the war; they were very close.

'Gabbin, do you hear me?' she shouted. 'Stay where you are – I'm coming.'

'Managu has gone, and the demons will get him,' he shouted.

Yola snorted. But then something in Gabbin's voice held her frozen for a second. Despite the blazing African sun a shiver passed down her back. What was it? What was making her uneasy? Then she knew – Gabbin had talked of demons! That, for him, was baby talk, back to the time during the war when Mother had used the threat of demons to keep them all away from dangerous places. There was only one place they all felt that there might be 'demons' and that was on the hill, and the hill was taboo. If Managu had gone up the hill …

She knew she ought to tell someone, but she couldn't betray Gabbin. Surely she could get Managu down for him. She looked around the compound – the high thorn hedge, grainstores, the three thatched huts where her mothers lived, Father's house – nothing stirred, no one had heard Gabbin calling. She would go on her own.

She ran lightly, ready with an excuse should anyone call out, until she was out of the compound, then she increased her speed, enjoying the cool draft of air in her face and the feeling of pushing the ground back under her feet. All during the war they had been cooped up in town while soldiers from both sides fought to possess this very hill. She was free to run now if she kept to the paths, but only the foolish, or the very brave, followed the narrow paths that led over the hill because when the soldiers had left they also left their booby traps and bombs all over it. People might know to keep to the paths, but a bull, hungry for the lush grass that grew on its slopes, never would.

She increased her pace again when she saw the cattle at the foot of the hill, where Gabbin, having raced back, was waving his stick to prevent the cows from following the distant call of their leader.

'Which way did he go?' she called as she ran up. Tears were streaming down the boy's face in black rivers.

'There, there, up past the Russian tank,' he sobbed. 'Get him back Yola, please!' Then he changed his mind, grabbed her hand and said, 'No, no, don't go, don't go. I don't want the Demon to get you.' His feet were pattering on the ground with anxiety as he was torn between the wish to go himself and the terrible taboo of the hill.

'Now, Gabbin,' said Yola, taking charge. 'I'm thirteen and a half, you're nearly ten. You keep the rest of the cows down here! Do you hear me? That's your job. That's a real man's job, understand? Don't worry, I will keep to the paths the grown-ups use every day, and there aren't really any demons, all right?'

Gabbin nodded, but his eyes were round with fear.

The Russian tank, looking evil, squatted in the grass like a rusted tin-can. The ragged hole that had finished it and killed the men inside gaped black. Yola knew it as a landmark, the edge of the safe ground, but it also showed the beginning of one of the illegal paths that people used to go over the hill. The path was narrow and she felt as if she were on a tight-rope as she tried to keep to the centre of it. Bushes, which had sprung up since the fighting had stopped, crowded in about her. She wondered why the path was so narrow, just wide enough for her feet. It was as if people had been afraid to put even a foot on the grass beside it.

The path wound on up the side of the hill, then divided. Yola stopped, her heart thumping harder than it should for such a little climb. The ridiculous talk about demons suddenly seemed real to her. She forced herself to examine the ground for hoofprints, but there was nothing to show which way Managu had gone. Flies buzzed, it was hot; she wanted to go down, get away from this hateful place. She saw a movement out of the corner of her eye and froze: a butterfly had momentarily opened its wings. This was stupid. Yola forced herself to breathe slowly and listened for the great bell that Managu wore around his neck. Yes, there! Surely that was it, down there below the path. She ran along, stretching to see over the bushes. The bell clanged somewhere below her now. She needed to be able to see; if only there were a rock or something she could climb on.

All at once the path widened and there was a tree spreading a pool of shade. It was a cinnamon tree, planted long ago by the white people for its spicy bark, which they used to flavour their food. People had rested here, a cigarette packet and a couple of Coke cans made that clear. At any rate the tree was what she had been looking for, she could climb it and see how to entice the bull to safety. The tree stood only a step from the resting place. She measured the distance to the lowest branch with her eye – it would be an easy jump and she was as agile as a monkey in a tree. She stepped off the path, treading lightly, and coiled herself for the jump. She didn't remember it afterwards, but as she jumped the ground gave under her ever so slightly; there was a tiny *click*.

For an eternity, in the flame of forty sunsets, she rose, thrown up and rag-dolled against the branch above. The upward blast from the landmine she had stepped on suspended her for a second, shook her as a terrier shakes a rat, then dropped her, pierced by her own bones, into the smoking pit where the mine had been laid. Spirits crowded her now, spirits of the dead jostling with spirits of the living, all fighting over the young life that she could feel pumping out of her before she lost consciousness. Her only other sensation, and the only one she would remember afterwards, was an overpowering scent of cinnamon.

◆ ◇ ◆

Gabbin stared at the hill; his jaw dropped and he trembled uncontrollably. The Demon had spoken! He watched as the small column of smoke that had spouted above the trees sagged and drifted away: the Demon's breath. A high, tremulous whimper began in his throat: 'Yola!'

The Demon would be coming for him now. It had no shape but many shapes, it was all the things that had ever terrified him: Grandfather in a rage, the forest at night, the cold, hard eye of a snake, the masks of the medicine men dancing in the flickering firelight and Mother's stories before she went away from him. It was coming! The echo of the blast bounced back from the hills around. It was reaching out for him. *Now*!

Gabbin turned to run, the skin on his back crawled at the thought of outstretched claws, the Demon's breath was on his neck. He collided with something huge and shrieked in terror. It was one of the cows. The cattle had moved up quietly behind him and were now standing in an interested half-circle, blocking his escape. Their heads were raised expectantly, their liquid brown eyes fixed on the hill behind him. Head down, Gabbin started to thrash and push through them, thrusting at them, fighting to get away. Warm, bony flanks towered above him, he beat against them with his fists, but it was no good. He turned and looked up the hill from within the safe stickle of the cow's horns. Slowly, his first panic was subsiding. He had responsibilities. Yes, *he* had been playing in the Russian tank. Yes, it was *he* who had let Managu climb into danger on the hill. Yes, *he* should have gone after him, but instead had called for Yola, a girl, and let her go onto the hill alone. What sort of a herd-boy was he?

✦ ✧ ✦

For an eternity, Gabbin knelt beside Yola under the cinnamon tree, pressing with all his might, his small hands finding by instinct the floodgate through which her life was draining away. And so he saved her life.

✦ ✧ ✦

Managu the bull emerged from the hill in his own good time, unscathed, unrepentant, and rejoined the herd. Gabbin was a hero – he had saved Yola's life; no one asked awkward questions about how Managu had got to be on the hill. Everybody gave him great praise, anything to draw his mind away from Yola's tragedy: let him be happy in believing that he had saved her life. But they talked in low voices to each other and Gabbin heard. He had grown up a lot in the last few hours. He had loved Yola, they all loved her – when Yola was happy everyone around her was happy. He had saved her, but now they were talking about her as if she had died. Who would give a bride-price for a girl on crutches or with a wooden leg? they were asking. What man would look twice at a girl whose only use would be to sit on a rock grinding maize? A girl with one leg can't work in the fields or carry water.

That evening, Gabbin looked up at the thatched ceiling above his bed, his face stiff from the tears that kept coming whenever he was alone. Finally, with a last deep sniff, he said to himself, 'Well, if nobody else will marry Yola, I will. I will have lots of wives, like Yola's father, but Yola will be the first and the best.' With this satisfying thought he slipped off into a demonless sleep.

2

The Night Mirror

Yola was running. She could hear Faran, one of her older brothers, laughing just behind her. She had tried to be clever and had dodged between the main hut and the granary, but now she realised why Faran was laughing: it was a trap. The others had cut her off. Gabbin was hopping up and down, yelling. In front of her was a circle of older women sitting on the ground; before them was spread a sheet with a neat pile of sorted millet seeds at the centre. 'Home' was the great tree at the centre of the compound. She decided to jump clean over both the sheet and the women. It would be a huge jump. She stepped back to increase her take-off, accelerated, coiled and sprang. As her foot pressed down on the ground, she felt it give slightly. As she was thrown skyward by the blast, she heard her own scream.

'Eeeh ... eeeh ... Quiet, child ... quiet ... you're all right. You're safe now.'

Yola realised that her mouth was open. Had she really screamed? Yes, her back was arched to scream again. She closed her lips tightly, but it became a silent scream, slicing through the hospital walls and racing like a jackal through the town. Past her home, up the hill where ghost soldiers from years ago hesitated in their work, spines chilled, suddenly uneasy, as the jackal passed by.

'Eeeh ... easy, my child ... relax ... it was just a dream.'

Gradually her back unbowed. Her mother was pressing a cup to her lips.

'I was jumping, Mother. I was jumping so high.' She paused. 'Mother ... my leg's hurting again.'

'It will love, they say it will. You must be brave.'

In the ceiling above her, a fan turned lazily, it moved the thick, hot air and stirred the frightening smells of the hospital. She watched a fly on one of its arms turning ... turning. It must be giddy, she thought.

Yola remembered very little about the drive to the hospital. Mother told her she had been taken on a moped. All she remembered was the smell of the man's sweatshirt; he was a mechanic and he smelt of oil. She was tied on to him in case she fell off. She drifted in and out of consciousness.

When they had arrived at the hospital, the doctor was cross. He was from a different tribe and was fuming and fussing in his own language. Was it her fault? But when he spoke to her in English, he was kind and said that he was just angry with the people who made landmines. She hadn't even known what a landmine was. She had asked him if Managu were safe, but he didn't seem to know who Managu was.

Someone in the ward said, 'Power cut.'

Yola was called back to the present. She looked up. The fan had stopped turning. The fly buzzed, spiralling down. She knew it would be giddy.

There'd been a power cut during her operation, too. She told the surgeon how she had woken to see them all crouched over her, faces masked, foreheads streaming with sweat, and how one of them had said, 'She's coming round.' The surgeon had laughed when she told him this.

'So you did wake? Yes, we had to put you to sleep again;

we've so little anaesthetic, I'm sorry. You see the lights went out for half an hour and I couldn't see a thing. Then they got the generator going. I'm afraid we didn't save your knee,' he added, smiling as he walked away.'

They all talked like that, as if she had no leg, but she could feel it. Let them talk, secretly she knew that her leg was still there. If she believed that it was there hard enough, then it would be. But when the doctors came to work on her, she closed her eyes tight, she could not look, she would not look! Yet the questions came.

'Which leg is it, Mother?' she whispered for the twentieth time.

'It's your left, chook.'

'It can't be Mother, I can still feel it. It feels like it's there.' Her mother mopped her forehead.

'The doctor says it will feel like that. He says you were lucky. Your body's not hurt.'

Yola noticed that Mother was crying quietly. She took her hand; it was rough with work. A surge of sympathy for that poor, worn hand tipped the balance – it was time for her to look at her leg. But how? There was a sort of basket over the foot of the bed, under the sheet. Probably to keep the weight of the sheet off her. It was no use looking to see how the sheet lay against her legs. She stared at the ceiling, grappling with the problem.

The fly had recovered from its giddiness and began to work its way up the window to where a small flap was tilted open for ventilation. Yola watched its passage to freedom. She was a prisoner. Was she going to spend the rest of her life staring at the ceiling, too frightened ever to look down at what might not be there? The power came on again and the fan resumed its lazy turning. Someone turned on the lights; night was turning the windows of the lighted ward into mirrors against the dark. The small window at the top was tilted at an angle, the fly had got to it and was walking about on its mirror surface. Yola noticed, looking at the reflection in the glass, that she could see the foot of her bed.

'Mother,' she whispered, 'the basket thing over my feet is uncomfortable. Could you take it off for a moment.'

Eyes tight shut, Yola wondered if she would be able to open her eyes when the moment came. She listened to her mother's movements as she stood and began to turn back the sheet. For a second, Yola hoped that perhaps Mother wouldn't bother to move the basket, but no, the basket was off and she could feel the movement of air against her skin. It was now or never.

She opened her eyes and stared up, gazing at the window, now a mirror above her. What she saw was confusing at first. She could make out her right leg, black against the sheet; she wriggled her foot. Then she looked to where her left leg should be. She thought she could see it, like a ghost, beside the other one. She blinked and the image was gone, leaving just white sheet. There was nothing, no leg at all – she couldn't understand, surely there was something left!

Gripping the side of the bed and summoning all her courage, she struggled to move what she still felt to be her left leg. Then at last she could see it! It was swathed in bandages, white against the white sheet, which was why she could not see it before. Bandages covered her thigh right down to where her knee should be. But there the bandages stopped. Like a great, soft, overpowering weight the full calamity of what had happened to her hit Yola.

✦ ✧ ✦

She had never been in a taxi before. It bounced and bucketed in and out of the potholes on the way from the hospital and she had to brace herself against the front seat with her crutches to avoid being thrown about. Mother sat in the back, leaning forward and shouting at the driver to be careful. For the last week, Yola had thought of nothing but coming home, imagining this moment, returning to her family, to normality at last. The taxi drew up outside the compound; the engine coughed to a halt and Yola could hear the blare of music coming from inside. There must be a party going on, that was Uncle Banda's ghetto blaster.

'Mother?' she began, feeling panicky now, but Mother had bustled in ahead of her. She heard the music stop in mid-beat. That's it – kill the music, she thought.

Yola leaned forward on her crutches, but for some reason her leg wouldn't follow. She tried again, but it just wouldn't move! It seemed to be rooted to the beaten earth. Nobody come out ... don't look! she willed as she struggled against ... what? Suddenly she realised that it was shame. She never felt shame! But this was different – it was shame of her body. In hospital everyone had been sick or injured, their injuries were often a source of pride and each new skill they learned a triumph. But now Yola felt naked. She had liked her body, it was a beautiful, strong body, but now it was spoiled and everyone would see that. She hadn't even thought to ask Mother to lengthen her dress.

She turned, she would go back to the hospital, back to where people without legs were normal. The taxi would take her. But where had it gone? It had slipped away and was already halfway down the hill, free-wheeling to save precious petrol.

At that moment she heard a cough and turned back. Gabbin stood in the compound entrance, standing very straight, with a new herdsman's spear at his side, a lethal-looking point glinting on the shaft. Someone had painted two white streaks on his cheeks – a boy's mark. Of course! he was now ten years old, and obviously taking his new status very seriously.

'Gabbin!' she exclaimed, 'I'm stuck!'

She had not seen him since her accident and wanted to hug him, but clearly for him this was some sort of ceremonial occasion. She quenched her grin, lowered her head as she would to someone very senior and made to move towards him. Fortunately, this time her leg obeyed her. With a stiff nod of acknowledgement, Gabbin turned and walked solemnly ahead of her into the compound.

They advanced slowly across the open space. Yola wondered what on earth was happening but, as is proper, kept the customary three paces behind her man. She glanced up briefly and out of the corners of her eyes saw that the compound was full of people. Why were they here, she wondered, but she focussed her eyes on where Gabbin was leading her.

In the very centre of the compound, under the great tree that had figured in her dream, sat Father in his robes on his ceremonial chair, his chief's fly-switch in his right hand. She had forgotten how frightening Father could look on formal occasions. The small noises about the compound died down. A baby cried, but that only added to the sense of quiet. Yola noted the knot of women – the gossips, as she called them – eyeing her closely. There were girls in the hospital who had been thrown out by their families. Perhaps this was how it happened.

Yola sensed everybody watching her, but tried to concentrate on Father and the two people seated on either side of him. Sister Martha was there on his right; she was headmistress of Yola's school. The little Irishwoman looked like an alert pink-and-grey parrot on a perch. Why was she here? On Father's other side sat Senior Mother, hunched like a vulture, eyes darting left and right.

Suddenly, from among the gossips, came a hoarse whisper, 'Who'd give a bride-price for that!'

Senior Mother whipped around with a hiss of disapproval. The comment had not been loud, but Gabbin had heard it. Yola nearly bumped into him – he had stopped rigid, drawing himself up to his full height. Then, as Father leaned forward to rise, Gabbin forestalled him. He took a step and lifted his spear. Senior Mother straightened sharply as Gabbin's voice rang out through the compound.

'Father,' said Gabbin, 'since Yola has lost her leg there are those who say no man will give you the money to make her his bride.'

Yola heard him – everyone in the compound heard him – his voice was clear and very definite. A movement like a sudden wind swept through the gathering. Everyone had been taken by surprise, not least of all Father, who was caught still in the act of rising. They all knew that Yola's life was ruined, that no one would give a price for a girl who could not dig, or work, or carry. They knew that her fate now was to grow old as a sort of perpetual aunt in the compound. But this wasn't the moment to speak or even hint at such things. There was a confused movement; people were uncomfortable. Gabbin must be stopped, but how to do it? A delicious tingle ran down Yola's back; something very special was happening. Father held up his hand, freezing the movements around the compound.

'Go on, Gabbin.' Father was now towering above him.

In a clear, challenging voice, Gabbin said, 'Father, when I am old enough, I will marry Yola. She will be my Senior Wife and my other wives will look after her.'

Yola nearly exploded. She wanted to stop him, and at the

21

same time to hug him; he was breaking every taboo imaginable! Had nobody told him? No boy could marry his first cousin, even as one of many wives. Then there was Sister Martha: she'd be horrified by the suggestion. The Catholic Church took a very serious view of men, even chiefs like Father, who had more than one wife. They had a name for it but she could not remember it. The compound was filled with a stunned silence. Yola was about to move forward when Sister Martha got up and addressed Father.

'Chief Abonda, you have here the perfect little Christian!' She turned to Gabbin, 'You wouldn't see your cousin stuck, would you, little man? I call that noble.'

Then, to Gabbin's obvious horror, she swept the terrified boy, spear and all, into her arms. Yola could imagine Gabbin's face. He'd hardly ever seen a white woman before, let alone been hugged by one. Eventually, Sister Martha released him; he looked shaken for a moment then recovered his dignity manfully. Please don't anyone laugh, Yola willed. A child clapped, the thin sound of small hands, then someone else took it up, and from there the clapping spread like fire in dry grass. Soon the whole compound was full of it. Not silly clapping, but real grown-up clapping. Gathering his dignity about him, Gabbin did an abrupt about-turn. For a split second, Yola's eyes met his and suddenly she understood: Gabbin knew that he could never marry her, but he had risked looking foolish in order to give them all a lesson in manners. He wasn't going to have people muttering against Yola.

The clapping faded, Yola turned and found that Father was standing in front of her. He looked into her eyes and for a second their minds seemed to touch – yes, she realised, he understood about Gabbin, too.

'People–' he began but halted. 'People of our tribe ...'

Suddenly, Yola realised he was fighting against uncontrollable laughter.

'People, look on our daughter, Yola, witness that we welcome her back into our family.'

At that he could get no further. Like a volcano erupting, he burst into laughter, shaking and mopping his eyes.

'Gabbin,' he roared, 'we'll make a chief of you yet.'

For a moment, Yola was engulfed in the folds of his robes. 'Well,' he chuckled in her ear, 'not all girls have an offer of marriage at thirteen. You'll make me rich yet.'

As he held her, the clapping changed to the happy roar of a party in full swing and, through and above the bellow of the ghetto blaster, Yola heard the shouts and yips of her friends. Father released her. A great weight seemed to lift from her; she threw herself forward on to her crutches and lurched across the compound towards them.

3

Sindu Mother

Being home was so wonderful after her stay at the hospital that Yola managed to bury deep any thoughts about the future. She lived from day to day and never noticed the black clouds of misery gathering until, one morning, she heard Shimima's voice calling. Yola was standing, hesitant between her crutches, pulled first one way and then the other by the sounds of the morning. This was the time when the women left to work in the fields. But she could not work in the fields; instead she had been left with a mountain of maize to grind.

'Ehhh, ehhh,' came the call of the women's voices. 'Are you going to the fields, sisters?'

'Yes, we are off to the fields so that our husbands can eat.'

'Yes, sisters. But who will you meet in the fields? Will the man of your dreams be hiding in the corn?'

'Quiet, sister! It is not just the corn that has ears.'

Laughter rippled through the cool morning air. Yola used to scorn these shouted jokes and conversations, called out over long distances as the women's paths crossed. The same each morning, meaningless ripples of sound and merriment, like pebbles thrown idly into a pool. But now they spoke to her of different things: of the freedom to walk the paths and work the fields and be part of the community of women: all pieces of a life that she, Yola, could no longer have.

The girl who had been speaking came into sight, a huge earthenware pot balanced on her head. It would have taken two other women to lift that pot on to her head at the well.

'Shimima,' Yola called, 'I see you.' She watched with a pang of jealousy as the girl, with the controlled grace of a giraffe, adjusted her pace and turned towards Yola without a splash from the pot.

'Ho, Yola, I see you. You are welcome back,' she called. 'Don't get into mischief on your own in the compound now.'

'Come and talk to me some day, Shimima,' Yola called, and she meant it. She'd always liked Shimima, a strong girl, older than she, who'd given up school to get married.

'I will when I haven't got the town's water supply on my head,' the girl called, laughing, beginning her slow turn back to the path.

'Your husband is lucky to have you.'

'I'll drown the layabout!' laughed Shimima happily. 'At least your husband won't be able to make you carry water for him. Make the most of it. I am walking.' At that she eased herself into a graceful walk again. Yola watched her go, the huge water pot seeming to float above her head.

'You are walking,' she called against a growing constriction in her throat. How could Shimima know that the one thing Yola wanted to do – and do right now – was to walk, like her, with a heavy pot of water on her head, away from the compound, away to someplace where there was a husband she could joke about, or to the North Pole, or to anywhere but here!

A group of children from up the valley passed by on their way to school. Would she ever get to school again? Her hopes had run high when she had seen Sister Martha at her homecoming party, but she knew that she could never manage the two miles to school on her crutches. Would she be stuck inside here forever? She looked around, and her mind turned to troubles closer to home. Trouble with her mothers.

She surveyed the compound. It was roughly circular, surrounded by a thick thorn hedge, broken on the downhill-side by the main entrance, which was a gap that could be closed at night with a thorn-reinforced gate. When you came into the compound, the first thing you saw was the great tree at its centre, with its welcome pool of shade. To the right of this was a square, mud-brick building with glass windows and an open porch – this was Father's house, where Senior Mother reigned supreme. When the electricity supply worked, Father had electric light and a television, which he would place on a table in the doorway for football matches; everyone would crowd around the door to watch the game.

During the day people came to discuss business with Father – he was the chief of the people who lived on the south side of Nopani, also he was a city councillor. Because she was a girl, Yola knew little about his business. She was keen on geography however, and knew all about her country. Nopani was the northernmost town in Kasemba, separated from Murabende, the country to the north, by the Ruri river. There was a bridge connecting Nopani to Murabende, but it was heavily guarded. Until recently, Murabende had supported the rebels, so their two countries had been close to war.

Father had three wives, each of whom had a hut of her own. First in importance was, of course, Senior Mother. Next came Yola's mother, who often acted as Father's secretary as she could speak English and type letters. Then, in a hut that still had fresh new thatch, lived Father's new wife, Sindu, a girl only a few years older than Yola. Yola grimaced, if Father had wanted a new wife why hadn't he chosen a nicer one? They'd been fine before she came. Yola suspected that her father chose his new wife to help Sindu's dad, who owed Father a lot of money. A generous bride-price from Father would cancel the debt. Perhaps Sindu would have preferred a younger husband? Even so, Yola's idea of a junior wife comprised a friend for her and someone to help Mother and Senior Mother with their work. Instead, from the very first day, Sindu seemed to resent Yola, seeing her as some sort of rival perhaps. At any rate, she seemed intent on making Yola into her slave while she lorded it around the compound.

Yola remembered her latest brush with Sindu; she hadn't really meant to insult her. It was the day of the party and Yola had been doing the rounds, talking and hugging and laughing with her friends; then she came on the 'Mothers'. These were all the older women and their friends, talking like hens, scratching and clucking over the town gossip as if someone had kicked open an ants' nest for them. There in the circle was Sindu, licking her dry little lips, trying to look twice her age and picking and scratching with the best. Yola knew she ought to say something polite. Later she told herself that it had been one of Gabbin's little demons that had got into her. She greeted Senior Mother without mishap.

'Senior Mother, I have returned. Ladies, I see you.' She bowed and smiled.

'We see you Yola, and are glad to see you back,' they chanted.

But it was the way Sindu chanted with them like an old crone that got into Yola and let loose the demon. Damn it! the girl was only a few years older than her. All Yola had said was, 'Hi, Sindu. How's the babies?'

She meant it – really meant it, as she told herself afterwards

– as just a little jibe at the way Sindu always chose to mind the babies when there was hard work to be done. But that wasn't what the demon had in mind. Sindu had no children of her own, no babies, not even a bulge, and this was a cause of great shame to her. The circle of ladies froze, sitting in mid-peck as if mesmerised by a snake that had suddenly slid into their midst. Yola froze too, unable either to speak or move; she had gone too far. Senior Mother, who had been sitting aloof, stirred ominously. If Yola had been younger or had not lost her leg, she was sure she'd have been beaten; but Senior Mother chose reconciliation.

'Do not greet your Mother Sindu with "Hi"', Yola. But I believe you mean well.' The old woman's eyes flashed up at Yola; she knew a demon when she saw one. 'Sindu will be glad of your help with the children now that you are back.'

Yola wanted to show her thanks, but the matter was closed. Senior Mother gathered her wrap around her and hunched up her shoulders, looking more like a vulture than ever. Yola realised she was dismissed and she backed away awkwardly. The hooded lids stayed down, but she had seen a glint in those eyes; Senior Mother understood her.

Apart from Senior Mother, who was scary, Uncle Banda seemed to be the only other interesting person in the compound, but he was in disgrace. He had fought with the rebels during the civil war; Father, of course, had supported the government. Uncle Banda was supposed to have surrendered his rifle when the rebels lost, but he hadn't. One day, Mother caught him teaching Gabbin how to aim it and she had made such a fuss that he had to hand it in to the police. He was Gabbin's godfather, so when Gabbin's parents died in the war he became Gabbin's legal guardian. Yola loved him, he was funny and wonderfully unpredictable – but even Yola had to agree

28

that he was a bad influence on Gabbin.

Now the excitement of coming home was a thing of the past – nothing about life in the compound was interesting. She lowered herself to the ground with a sigh, her leg to one side of the grindstone, her stump to the other. She placed a pad of cloth under her stump as it was still very tender. She sat at the grindstone as she had on the day of her accident. Perhaps she could start the story again. When little Gabbin starts calling, this time she will reassure him and tell him that Managu can find his way down from the hill on his own. All Gabbin has to do is to stay with his cows. Then she will be able to run again … *Stop*! She hammered the grinder down on the maize. Why did all her daydreams end with her running?

She looked at the grinder, a rounded stone that fitted neatly in the hand – pity it hadn't broken the grindstone! She steadied herself, brushed back the grain she had scattered and started the rhythmic swing of grinding. To begin with, the stone rumbled and grumbled over the grain, then, slowly, it began to move more smoothly over the ever-fining flour. Back and forth, back and forth, back and forth her body moved.

The compound fence rose around her higher and higher, crowding in on her like a prison wall. Her future held nothing but this *crish* … *crish* … *crish*.

She heard the sound of the approaching vehicle through the rumble of her grinding. No vehicles came beyond the town on this road, not since an anti-tank mine had wrecked a timber lorry a mile outside the town. She was staring in the direction of the noise when she saw the car's aerial – to her it was a long, thin pole whipping backwards and forwards above the hedge as the car lurched up the hill. She stared, wondering what it could be. She saw Sindu appear at the door of her hut, cocking an ear at the sound. Yola listened, spellbound, her hands white, the maize flour a glistening peak on the mat in front of her. She was like a prisoner hearing, with sudden hope, footsteps approaching and keys chinking. She had to know what this new sound meant ... she had to see ... she had to be there. In a minute it would be gone – quick! She rolled over and grabbed at her crutches, scrabbling in the dirt like a wounded bird trying to get up. Once up, she tried to run, but then lost her rhythm and nearly fell. Sindu was running ahead, trailing a comet-tail of toddlers ready to tangle in Yola's crutches. For just a second, Yola saw the big car as it passed, its tyres spurting dust. She saw a uniformed driver, some writing on the door ... and it was gone. The long, thin pole mocked her over the fence; the car changed gear and ground on up the hill. Yola was immobilised by a grubby infant who was holding on to one of her crutches. She detached him and worked her way through the youngsters to the gate. All that remained was a cloud of dust where the car had been.

'Where were you? You should have seen it!' Sindu gasped, wide-eyed.

Yola pursed her mouth. Sindu knew perfectly well that she couldn't run, but Yola was determined not to react.

'You should have hurried,' tried Sindu again with a wicked little glance.

Yola would happily have taken a swipe at her, but the memory of Senior Mother's look on the day of the party sat on her shoulder like a vulture; she would be good.

'Who were they?' she asked.

'How would I know, they didn't stop to say.' Sindu's sarcasm was unmistakeable. This time Yola's frustration flared.

'But on the side. It was written! What did it say?'

The words had come out without Yola realising their significance. Sindu was looking at her like a knife looking for a set of ribs to slide through; Sindu could not read. Yola's demon had struck again, and having popped the words into her mouth, it scuttled off and left her to clear up. Wearily she said, 'Look Sindu, I'm sorry, but if only you'd let me help you I'd teach you to read.'

Sindu had never been to school, she didn't want to learn, and Yola had offered. Sindu walked away from her, towards the compound entrance. Yola, remorseful now, was determined to repair her bridges, so she called, 'I do mean it Sindu, it's really quite easy, we—'

She stopped in mid-sentence. Sindu wasn't listening. She was smiling and looking intently up into the compound.

'What's up, Sindu?'

'Oh Yola, trouble, trouble … chuck, chuck, chuck.'

Yola hitched herself forward urgently to see. Chickens were flocking and pecking all over her abandoned corn, wading through the ground flour, scattering it left and right.

'Well, don't stand there, run Sindu, chase them you cow!' she yelled, appeasement forgotten.

'Don't you dare talk to me like that. I'm your Mother, and don't forget it!'

Yola looked around for something to hit her with, fortunately thinking of her crutches too late. Sindu, however, saw the danger and hopped out of range.

'All right, all right, but only because you're a cripple.'

Yola tried a late swipe, missed and had to hop to find her balance.

'Temper!' said Sindu, and Yola could only sob with rage as the older girl walked slowly up the hill as if the exercise would kill her, waving her arms ineffectually.

◆ ◇ ◆

31

The next morning, Gabbin startled her by peering into the secret place she had between the granary and the compound fence. No one knew of this secret place apart from Gabbin. She kept her precious school books here in a battered tin-box, safe against the ants. Since her accident she had been escaping in here whenever she could, just to pretend she was still at school, and, more significantly, to get away from Sindu. But Gabbin was not coming in today.

'Yola! Shhh. They are coming.'

He was literally vibrating with excitement. She had been miles away, wondering what snow would feel like, poring over grainy pictures of dogs and sledges in her geography book.

'Come in, Gabbin. You might be seen.'

'It's Landcruiser men! That went past yesterday. They are going up the hill, quick quick quick or you'll miss them!'

'What are they doing? Why ...' but Gabbin was turning to run.

'The hill, Yola, they are going to hunt the demons from the hill!' His lapse into baby talk was accidental. 'Landmines,' he called as he pelted down towards the entrance, the pink soles of his feet flashing.

Yola dropped everything and, thanks to Gabbin, was ahead of everyone else, swinging through the entrance just as the Landcruiser rose through the heat shimmer towards her. She heard Sindu's flat-footed run behind her and didn't care.

'Where have you been? I've been looking for you every-where.'

'Busy,' snapped Yola, without turning.

'I think I'll stop them. I could tell them where you found the landmine,' said Sindu.

Yola clenched her teeth. 'Don't you think *I* could tell them that better than you,' she muttered.

'What was that? Oh look, there's a white man!' said Sindu, waving excitedly. Yola had been about to wave herself, but she was sickened by Sindu's cavortions and concentrated on the writing on the car door: Northern People's Aid, she read. Eskimos! she thought, and a rare bubble of laughter rose inside her. She looked up and found herself smiling happily into the eyes of the man in the car. He seemed surprised but smiled back at once. Then the car had gone past and Yola realised she had never smiled at a white man before. But why had he been looking at *her* so intently? Then she remembered her crutches and her ugly stump. Her lingering smile faded. She turned to go back into the compound but she was knee-deep in children. Behind her, she heard the car slow down, then a high whine as it reversed. She couldn't move and she wasn't going to turn to face them – at least the children were shielding her leg – so she faced stubbornly into the compound. She heard voices, then Gabbin's voice, high and triumphant.

'No, not you Sindu – it's Yola he wants.'

She had to turn then. Gabbin looked tiny beside the jeep, but nevertheless completely in charge of the situation.

'Come on Yola, he wants to talk to *you*!'

Sindu was walking towards her with a face like sour milk. Yola avoided her eyes, and a subtle little sideswipe at her crutch, as she lurched over towards the car. The man swung the car door wide open and her leg felt very exposed; she felt suddenly shy and had to force herself to look up. To her surprise, the man was not staring at her leg, he was smiling at her, one eyebrow raised as if he liked what he saw.

'The young chief here tells me you speak good English.'

'A little,' Yola lied, dropping her gaze.

Then, to her surprise, the man shot his hand out towards her and said, 'Hans. I'm Hans.'

She looked at his hand. What should she do? She had to balance while she freed her hand from her crutch in order to take his; it felt warm and strong. She had thought a white man's hand would be soft and flabby. He had a tousle of short fair hair and blue eyes. Sister Martha had blue eyes too, so Yola was no longer disturbed by them. This man's eyes seemed to be laughing.

'My name is Yola,' she said, trying not to giggle; the dark thoughts that had been plaguing her lifted like a cloud drifting away from the sun.

He talked to her quietly, while she stood listening intently. He asked about her accident, where it had happened and how she was managing with the crutches. He talked so naturally, and seemed to know so much, that soon it felt as if it were not shameful for her to have only one leg. He told her about people he knew who had artificial legs, false limbs so clever that you could hardly tell them from the real thing. He went on to tell her how they had come to find and clear away the landmines about the town. All the time, Gabbin stood beside her looking up, eyes switching back and forth between them, struggling to understand with his few words of English. They were all so engrossed that no one noticed when Sindu slipped away from the small crowd that had gathered about the vehicle.

'I mustn't keep you standing,' the man said eventually. 'Also, we have work to do. Tomorrow, perhaps you would like to come up to see what we are doing?'

Before she had time to think, Yola nodded in agreement. It was only when the Landcruiser had roared off that she realised how frightened she was at the thought of going anywhere near that hill again.

✦ ✧ ✦

Sindu was waiting for her when she got back into the compound. To her surprise, she smiled and asked if Yola could possibly look after the little ones as she had an errand to do. Because of this, Yola forgot to go back to her secret place to put her books away.

4

Demons!

Mr Hans pulled up outside the compound early the next morning. Yola was waiting, her fears had subsided and she longed, even for one day, to get out of the compound. Also, she was curious about Mr Hans.

'I must ask your mother,' he insisted. 'She will think I have abducted you.'

Yola had no idea what abducted meant, but she understood enough to send an excited Gabbin flying off.

'*My* mother!' she shouted after him. 'Not–'

Gabbin turned with an impish grin and did a perfect imitation of Sindu's flatfooted walk, before scuttling off into the compound. Surely Mother would let her go. She could almost feel the thorns of the hedge encircling the compound reaching out to draw her back into it again. When Mother appeared, Mr Hans took her to one side; Yola and Gabbin just had to watch and hope. Mother's English was perfect; she had worked as a secretary with an English company before the civil war. Ever since Yola could remember, Mother had spoken to her in English when at home – it was a private language for them. Mother had always said it would help Yola to get a job, but what Yola really wanted to do was travel.

When Mr Hans came back he looked solemn and shook his

head. 'Your mother says that you can come, but that you must have a man with you to protect you.'

Yola was dumbfounded. What could he mean – a man? She turned to Mother, but Mother was staring innocently at Mr Hans. Yola, sensing a conspiracy, whipped around. Sure enough the white man was grinning, then he glanced sideways at Gabbin.

'Mother,' Yola said in English, 'can Gabbin come with me to protect me from this dangerous white man?'

'If he agrees,' Mother replied.

There was a whirr and a scurry and Gabbin was climbing into the Landcruiser like a spider. 'Keep an eye on him,' she said.

'How did he understand?' asked Yola in amazement.

'Because he's a bright lad – he knows more English than you think,' said Mr Hans.

On the way, Mr Hans talked about his work: how the NPA used mine detectors to find the mines and then destroyed them.

'One of the most important things we do Yola, is what is called mines awareness. You see, people – particularly children – don't know about mines and how dangerous they are. We aren't very good at telling them because we don't speak the languages of the tribes and we don't know the sorts of problems local people have, like where they go for water, or how they get to their fields. Because of this we like to train local people to give mines awareness classes. Someone like you, who has suffered from a mine, would be ideal. People would see that you have lost a leg and would listen to you as they would never listen to me or to someone they think knows nothing about it. That's why I wanted to talk to you and to show you what we are doing. Perhaps you might be interested?'

Yola could hardly believe what she was hearing. She stared

ahead as the Landcruiser pitched and rolled up the hill. She was afraid to say yes in case she hadn't understood correctly, but her whole body was shouting *Yes!* Away from Sindu, away from the compound, away into something new. She would take Gabbin with her, then she wouldn't have to feel uneasy about Uncle Banda and his Kalashnikov rifle.

'Could Gabbin help?' she asked.

'Well, he's a bit little, isn't he, and he doesn't have enough English yet. I want him to see what we are doing up here for his own safety and because he will influence his friends. I don't want to press you, but think about it.'

Press her! Yola felt like throwing her arms around him – but at that moment she saw the hill, and a sudden fear froze her in her seat. Staring through the windscreen it seemed that it was the hill, rather than the car, that was tossing about as they approached up the uneven road. Her tongue was dry and sticky in her mouth. Up there was the path – the tree – she'd not been back since that day. What if she failed, what if she turned and ran? She swallowed painfully on nothing and clamped her mouth shut.

Mr Hans reached up to help her down from the jeep. There she stood. What if mines had been laid down here too? The earth below the cinnamon tree had looked as innocent as this. She stood there miserably. Now, of all times, when she most needed to be brave, she was frozen with fear. It was all coming back to her. Would every step feel like this? How could she teach mines awareness when she dared not take even a single step herself? A small hand crept around the grip on her crutch to take hold of her thumb. Gabbin, too, was remembering. Mr Hans was looking at them. An apologetic smile and a shrug was all she could manage. This would be the end of his offer.

'Frightened?' he asked. 'We all feel it, you know. Come,

Yola, translate for me. Tell Gabbin in Kasembi that it is good to feel afraid because then you can be safe.'

Yola whispered the translation and felt Gabbin's grip tighten on her thumb. Hans went on.

'Your job, Gabbin, is to warn people not to be foolish and not to go where they know there may be mines, and never to play with things they find, no matter how harmless they look. If your friends find anything suspicious they should come to us and, if it is dangerous, we will destroy it. They will listen to you because you are a hero – you saved your sister's life.' He turned to Yola. 'Yola, you will always be frightened, but being frightened will protect you and it will get less, I can assure you. We will teach you where it is safe to go and where it is not.'

'But I can't see them. There might be one right here, now, under my foot,' she whispered.

'Ya, see Yola, you are already asking the right question: *Is this place safe?* Well, I can tell you that it is because we have checked it.'

But Yola wasn't convinced. 'It is like lying in your hut at night wondering if there is a snake in the thatch,' she said.

'Yes, that would be frightening, but what if you can see the snake, what will you feel then?' Mr Hans asked.

'More frightened, but I will know where it is then. I can run away. One of the men can kill it if it is dangerous!'

'So, the real danger comes not from the snake but from not knowing where it is.'

'I suppose so.'

'That's why we are here, Yola. Our job is to find mines and, when we know where they are, destroy them. The mines themselves need not be frightening. Let me show you what a land-mine looks like.'

Yola moved forward as if in a dream. She knew that she was

safe with Mr Hans, but what about her demons? They were after her, and from Gabbin's tight grip she knew that they were after him, too.

A piece of ground had been marked off with red-and- white tape; a triangular notice declared, *Danger: Landmines*. Lined up on the ground behind the sign were things that looked like rusty cans of beans and tins of boot-polish. It was the sort of display she used to make when she had played 'shop' as a child. But these were not empty cans. Mr Hans stepped over the tape.

Yola stepped back involuntarily. Hans bent down and lifted up one of the little cylinders. Without further warning, Yola's demons ran amok in her mind. Hans's voice came to her echoing from a great distance.

'This mine has been made safe, Yola, so I can open it and show you.' Open it? Open again that dreadful day so carefully sealed?

'Yola … Yola … Managu has gone up the hill,' Gabbin was calling again.

The mine lay in two halves now, open like an oyster in Hans's hands, and Managu's bell was clanging on the hill below. If only she could see!

'It works like this. When someone steps on the mine the top collapses in and presses down on this trigger in the middle here.' Hans's finger moved with elaborate slowness towards the tiny plunger rising like a tower in the centre of the mine. Yola closed her eyes. A butterfly opened its wings. She heard the *click* as the plunger struck home. The butterfly took off in alarm. Together they fluttered in random spirals above the hill.

'The trigger sends a spark down this red wire to the detonator.'

The column of smoke was snaking quietly towards the sky. A crumpled figure lay beneath a cinnamon tree, a thread of red spreading on the brown earth. Where is Gabbin? Hurry, hurry, Gabbin.

'The detonator is this thing that looks like the stub of a pencil. The explosive can't go off without it.'

The butterfly must have delivered her to hospital because now she is in bed and they have come to change her bandages. This time she will look, not at her reflection in the night mirror, but really look. She props herself up on her elbows.

'You can see how the detonator nestles into this white putty-like stuff. That's the explosive!'

There was her stump, unbandaged, stitched and raw, stretched like a detonator in the folds of white sheet. The world began to turn and Yola was looking up not at Mother but at Hans. A black veil like drifting rain was falling between them. His voice was getting fainter. And there was a smell in her nostrils, spicy, familiar, overpowering: the scent of cinnamon.

The sudden breeze in her face was welcome. Yola opened her eyes to a blur of movement. Hans was fanning her with his hat, a look of alarm and consternation on his face. She smiled, and the look of alarm was replaced with one of relief.

'I'm sorry ... so sorry ... it was insensitive of me. I should have known it would be upsetting for you. I'll take you home.'

What had happened? Yola wondered. Where was Gabbin? They had been holding hands.

'Is Gabbin all right?'

'Oh he's fine, he's right here.'

Yola probed her mind like someone feeling to see if she's been injured, but the demons were gone, her mind lay open – like an oyster. She smiled at Hans, his frantic flapping was easing.

'Please, Mr Hans. I'm all right now, please don't take me home.'

❖ ◇ ❖

That evening, Yola lay in the wide bed she shared with her

mother and talked and talked. She talked about her visit to the hill, about the ghosts that had come back to haunt her, about hospital and about school. Mother said nothing, just 'eeh … eeh', which meant that she was listening but not forming an opinion either. That was a nice thing about Mother, she didn't say anything if she had nothing to say, just eeh … eeh. It was a comforting sound and eventually Yola found herself drifting off into sleep. She had said nothing to Mother of Hans's suggestion about her teaching mines awareness. That could wait. Curled against the crook of Mother's back, she dreamed about Hans.

✦   ✧   ✦

In the morning, when the other children had left for school, Yola slipped back into her secret place between the granary and the compound fence to think. Some time ago, when she discovered that she could no longer squat with only one leg, Gabbin had helped her to bring a log in to sit on. She sat down and rested her forehead on her knee. She wanted to think, but she couldn't get comfortable or settled; something was out of place. She tried again. What was it that Hans had said? Oh yes, that her school work should come first. How could he know that she could never go to school again? All she had were her books. If only she could get to school … Suddenly, Yola stiffened and her scalp began prickling. Her school books! She had left them here, scattered. When was that? Oh no! It was the day before yesterday. And her tin-box. She slewed around left and right, but the books had disappeared. She poked in the gap in the hedge where she kept her tin-box, but it was empty. Could Gabbin have taken them? Could he have cleared them up for her? No one else knew about this place, it must be him … but was it? For a crazy moment she thought that Sindu might have found her secret place and taken them, but Sindu couldn't read, and as they had already had a row over that she didn't like to ask her. Nevertheless, as black depression settled over Yola, a small worm of suspicion worked itself down deep inside her.

Days passed, the Landcruiser ground up the hill each morning and did not stop. Mr Hans had forgotten about her; she couldn't go to school; she had lost her books and Gabbin swore that he had not touched them. There didn't seem to be anything to look forward to. She had a party to mark her fourteenth birthday, but it was a gloomy affair.

✦　✧　✦

It was the time of year for planting maize, when the ground was still moist after the rains. The seed corn had been taken from the granary, and the back-breaking job of planting the maize was about to begin. Yola wasn't surprised when Sindu volunteered to look after the children, leaving Yola the even less enjoyable task of picking stones out of the millet for the midday meal. The millet grains were tiny and so were the stones, which had been picked up during thrashing. In the end, it really meant hand-picking each millet grain from one pile and placing it on a clean pile on a separate cloth. Yola had learned long ago to put herself into a sort of trance when doing boring jobs like this. In her imagination she would travel the world ... who could have taken her geography book? she wondered. She didn't mind so much about the others, but the geography book, with its photographs of the world, was where she got her ideas for her imaginary journeys – it was her passport to the world – and she needed it now! The pile of picked grains grew from a mound to a cone. She looked up and found Hans smiling down at her.

'Where were you? I could have shouted and you wouldn't have heard me?' he said.

'I didn't hear your car.' She was surprised into resentment – why hadn't he come before?

'I walked down from the hill.'

'Oh, I didn't think ...'

'... that Europeans walked anywhere,' he laughed. 'Why aren't you at school?'

Yola shrugged and nodded towards her stump. 'It's too far to walk.'

'But you *must* go to school!' He seemed quite shocked. 'We *need* you to go to school!'

Yola shrugged. She wasn't sure of her English. Why would *he* need *her* to go to school? Hans squatted down awkwardly. She'd heard that Europeans couldn't squat properly, with feet flat on the ground.

'Look, Yola,' he said, 'I want to ask you again. We would like you to help us with our mines awareness programme, remember? People, kids particularly, will listen to you.'

'Because of this?' and she tipped her chin towards her stump.

'No! Because you're bright, and you're pretty, and you know what it's like to suffer. Please Yola, I didn't like to ask you last time. Remember, you'd been upset?'

She looked down at her cone of millet seeds and shook her head.

'Was that yes, or no?' he asked.

She looked him directly in the face, flaring bitterly. 'I'd like to help you. I'd like to go back to school. I'd like to visit the Eskimos, perhaps even visit the moon, but I have work to do.' She gestured towards the growing pile of millet seeds. Her lower lip was beginning to tremble. 'For maths I can count seeds, for English I can make up stories, for mines awareness I can look after babies.' She resumed her sorting, biting her treacherous lip. It was all right for him with his big car and his complicated-looking watch. She felt a tear on her cheek, but she didn't want to draw attention to it by wiping it away.

Perhaps the man hadn't understood her. He squatted there uncomfortably, watching the seeds falling on the pile, saltating down the slopes. A small landslide would change the profile of the cone from time to time. Then he did a surprising thing: he reached out and touched the tear that was progressing slowly down her cheek.

'We must do something about this, Yola,' he said and clambered to his feet, his knees emitting some alarming snaps. He turned then and strode out of the compound.

Next day, the older children walking back from school reported that the deminers' car had called at the school, and that Sister Martha had spent a whole hour talking to the man with blue eyes.

✦　✧　✦

'Sindu?' Yola called. 'Sindu mother?'

No answer. She'd been there a moment ago. Yola's mother wanted to borrow an extra pot; Yola ducked her head and went into Sindu's hut. It was sparsely furnished. A curtain hung across the room to one side, concealing the bed.

'Sindu?' Yola called again.

Against the back wall was a table with a coloured cloth over it and a mirror. On the right of this was a radio, on the left was ... Yola's tin-box. Yola froze. Her first reaction was to back out, forget it, avoid confrontation, but her feet didn't move. Then she tried making excuses – perhaps Sindu had rescued them for her? The books had after all been left out in the open. But Sindu didn't know about her secret place.

As if drawn by a magnet, Yola crossed the room and lifted the lid. The shock was electric. The books were gone, no rubber, no pencil, nothing but someone else's knick-knacks! This was *her* box, home for *her* treasured things. This was a violation, like finding something crawly in your clothes. In one compulsive movement she spilled the contents out, recognising a string of beads that Sindu had worn when she had first arrived, some seashells from the coast and a man's watch, obviously not working. They all scattered on the floor. Yola clutched the tin to her, swivelling awkwardly on her crutches. *Where were her books?*

There wasn't much light in the hut. Yola squinted. On the opposite side of the room was the corner where Sindu parked the babies when she had charge of them. There were the books! Yola pounced, dropping the tin-box with a clang. They were already torn and crumpled, two – no – three. But no geography book! Hope. Where was her geography book, her passport, it must be somewhere here? She searched frantically, poking with her crutches, churning through broken toys. Unless … unless … she swivelled around, lurched across the hut and pulled at the curtain shielding the bed. It came away in her hand and billowed about her, clinging to her leg and her crutches. There, decorating the walls above the bed, was page after page of her precious book. There were her Eskimos! Rage blazed behind her eyes. She tried to reach across the bed but she couldn't. Perhaps she screamed, perhaps it was Sindu's scream from the door that rang through the compound, but suddenly they were facing each other across the crumpled curtain like rival leopards.

'What are you doing in here!' Sindu yelled. 'Look at my bed, look at what you have done!' She rushed at Yola, but Sindu did not know the extent of Yola's fury. They met in a tangle of curtain. Yola managed to push the older girl back and put all of her energy into shouting.

'How dare you take my books! I've lost my leg, I've lost my freedom, I've lost any chance of being married like you, I can't even go to school, and you've torn them up.'

She was aware of shouts from outside. Sindu obviously heard these too and put her head back and screamed – no words – just screaming. This was too much for Yola, all her restraint blew away. She freed one of her crutches and hit Sindu as hard as she could, first on the shoulder and then, when she was turning, across the back. Her crutch broke with a snap and Yola was helpless.

The door darkened as people came crowding in. Sindu was helped out of range and Uncle Banda edged around to get behind Yola, afraid of a belt from a crutch himself. Before she realised what was happening, Yola's arms were pinned to her sides and she was lifted up bodily and carried out the door. Sindu made a rush at her, but someone held her back. This time, Yola had gone too far.

5

Trial and Sentence

For two days, Yola was confined to her mother's hut. No one came near her. Her food was brought to her on a banana leaf, as if they thought she would throw her plate at someone. Mother came and went, slept and was silent. Yola realised she was in deep trouble. She followed the activity in the compound by the sounds she heard. Her hopes lifted when she heard the deminers' car. She even heard Mr Hans's voice in the distance, but hoped he wouldn't try to see her. She was also sure that she had heard the putter of Sister Martha's moped, but that was unlikely.

On the third day her mother, her own precious mother, came to talk to her. She asked Yola to tell her everything – about her books, about how Sindu had been treating her. When Yola was hoarse from talking she asked, why all these questions? That afternoon, she was told, Father would sit in judgement and Mother, as Yola's true mother, would have to make Yola's case.

'Why not me?' Yola asked.

'It is better this way,' was all her mother would say.

Yola washed and dressed with care, not that she had many clothes to choose from. The solemnity of the occasion became clear when her friends were allowed in to help her with her

48

hair, parting it, plaiting it, even working in some modest beads.

'What's going to happen?' she wanted to know, but they kept quiet, as if they'd been told to say nothing. Uncle Banda came in with a pair of new crutches that he had made for her. They were a bit long, but there would be no time to shorten them.

'I've made them extra strong,' he said, as she tried them.

'Why strong? Have I put on weight since I've been locked away in here?' Yola asked.

'No, it's so that next time you take a swipe at Sindu, the crutch won't break.'

Yola couldn't believe it; she was quite shocked. She had come to accept her guilt and shame and here was Uncle Banda … she could feel a laugh – no, worse, a giggle rising. She must not giggle! If she giggled in front of everybody it would be terrible. This was so like Uncle Banda. Just when you thought you knew where you were with him, he did something surprising. Like siding with the rebels when everyone else was against them. Footsteps were approaching. Uncle Banda's voice changed.

'I hope you're thoroughly ashamed of yourself!' he said, loud enough for anyone to hear.

Yola didn't dare look at him. But it was just one of her friends; she poked her head through the doorway. 'Sindu's gone in,' she said, and Yola was left on her own again. Why is it taking so long? she wondered.

Yola halted at the doorway to Father's house. She was propped between her too-long crutches, head bent forward. On her way down she had passed Sindu, who was leaving. If Sindu looked as if she had received a life sentence, what was going to happen to Yola? Sindu had muttered spitefully, 'Now you're for it!' but it was a half-hearted effort.

Why had Father elected to use his house, rather than the big tree, to sit in judgement? Yola wondered. She blinked in the dim light as she stepped in through the door. Then she blinked again: Sister Martha and – of all people – Hans were there! Uncle Banda was part of the semicircle around Father's chair, together with several elders from the neighbourhood; she'd expected that, but not the white people. Oh God! Yola's mother was standing back; she'd had her say. Senior Mother was there, not part of the circle, but a source of invisible power in the gloom. All eyes were on Father.

As Yola walked forward they all looked around at her, but she could glean nothing from their expressions. She had been rehearsing all the things she would say against Sindu; suddenly they no longer seemed so important. Father sat, not saying a word, just looking at Yola steadily, as if his face were carved from ebony. The last of her truculence ebbed away. The biting things and pert comments soaked out through the soles of her feet into the polished earth of the floor. Why were Sister Martha and Mr Hans here to see her shame? She had so wanted to please them, and now …

Father began to speak. His voice came deep from his chest as if rising up through him from the earth. Yola struggled to understand because he was not using their everyday language: he spoke the language of their people when they talk of sacred things – matters of the tribe, matters of law and the spirit – a ritual language that flows like a deep river. To Yola's surprise, he was not speaking about her but seemed to be telling a story. It was a story about a girl who had nothing, no education, little food, no possessions, and whose family had fallen on hard times. After a little, Yola found she was no longer listening with the top of her mind, but was letting his words sink in like water on dry soil, penetrating into parts of her she did not even know existed. Images began to rise in her mind, unbidden. She saw the face of a girl, only a little older than herself, vaguely familiar, a stupid face, but tear-stained and miserable. It dawned on her that it was Sindu's face, but from some time ago.

A man's voice rasped. 'You *will* do as I say!' Then, rising to a scream, 'You are *mine* to give away! I'll never get a better offer for you. Just look at your snivelling face!'

'But Juvimba?' the girl sobs.

'That rebel! He couldn't even pick the winning side! He's still mixed up with them, I hear. All he'd give me for you would be a stick of dynamite. Probably all you're worth! Don't talk to me about him ever again!'

'But I'll be lonely.'

'Of course you won't. No third wife is ever lonely.'

The weak, feckless voice raved on. But Yola was seeing Sindu's meagre possessions again: some cheap beads, seashells – her one visit to the sea probably – and a man's watch that did not work – Juvimba's? Suddenly they were scattered on the floor.

'No!' she exclaimed, jolting as if waking from a dream.

Father's face materialised. Had she exclaimed aloud? As if he understood, his voice changed. The ritual chanting was gone and she realised he was speaking in English, slowly and clearly so that Sister Martha and Mr Hans could understand.

'Now we come to your punishment, Yola my daughter, and this is how it must be understood by everyone outside these walls. I have decided that you are to be banished from this compound for striking your mother, Sindu. Do you accept my decision?'

Yola felt herself swaying on her crutches. Was this it, was she too to be married off? What did banished mean? She searched

Father's face but there was no answer there. Then she stood up as straight as she could and said, 'Yes, Father.'

A ripple of movement, like wind in the grass, spread through the people in the room. Yola knew that it wasn't her place to speak but she had to.

'Father, I am sorry–' she began, but immediately Father stiffened.

'Quiet girl! Do you think that I have been talking to you for all this time without knowing your mind? Do you think I am a mask that you can look at without it knowing you? You and I have been on a journey together, now we must see if you are capable of learning from it. I have spoken. Now, Sister Martha and Mr Eriksen will tell you about our plans for you.'

Yola sat in her secret place – not so secret now, but still a place to come. Gabbin came in and sat for a little while, hoping for information, but she wasn't giving any. She sent him away while she tried to absorb what they had said. Sister Martha had looked like a little grey parrot, while Mr Hans tried to look serious. She went over her sentence again, this time pretending she was on trial in a real court.

'Criminal Yola Abonda, this is your sentence,' they might have said. 'You are banished from this compound, banished from the city of Nopani, banished even from Kasemba, your country. You will be taken from here (in chains, perhaps), and despite your protests you will be given some beautiful new clothes. You will then be put on an aeroplane and flown to your place of exile – a small island off the coast of Western Europe.'

At first, Yola thought that he had said Iceland rather than Ireland. 'Eskimos?' she had asked. But Mr Hans explained that even in Iceland she mightn't see Eskimos. What she would see in Ireland, however, was lots of rain. Sister Martha had been quite indignant and said it was the island of a thousand greens and everyone had laughed.

'Silence! Criminal Yola,' the judge would have continued, 'there you will be taken to a place of correction where the leg you so carelessly lost will be replaced and made as good as new. After that you are sentenced to school with extra geography lessons because you don't know the difference between Iceland and Ireland!'

Yola would be away for nearly a year. She would spend two or three weeks in hospital while she was given her new leg, and then a whole year at a convent school belonging to Sister Martha's order.

She leant back and looked up at the little patch of blue through the leaves above her and felt that she already had wings. She wanted to shout and tell her friends and to laugh and sing, but she wouldn't. Father had taken her on a journey and trusted her. She decided that, when the time was right, she would give Sindu the remains of her geography book, all that is but one picture – her picture of the Eskimos, that she would probably keep forever.

✦ ◇ ✦

Yola began to lead a double life. Inside the compound she was palpably in disgrace. Senior Mother seemed to be everywhere, like a watchful vulture ready to hop in at the slightest sign of trouble. Yola wanted to see Shimima, but she had always been busy when the girl had passed by. Then, a couple of days after her 'trial', she heard a voice calling.

'Eheeeh? … Yola Abonda, I hear great things of you!'

Yola emerged from her hut, where she'd been bruising herself trying to sweep with one hand. Shimima, on her way to the well this time, had placed her great water jar beside the gate.

Kasembi is a language meant for calling out, and Shimima had a fine, strong voice.

'Ehee ...!' Yola called in return, but snipped it short; Senior Mother had appeared at the door of Father's house and was glaring at the unfortunate Shimima. Yola abandoned her sweeping brush and swung her way down towards her friend, anxious to head off trouble and trying to force her face into some semblance of seriousness. She had to pass Senior Mother on the way; bright eyes watched from under hooded lids. Yola prayed that she would be allowed to pass when, in little more than a whisper, Senior Mother spoke.

'I'm glad for you Yola, Shimima is a good girl. Go with her, but keep your laughter till later. Remember, here you are in disgrace.'

For a second the lowered lids lifted – a suggestion of a smile, but a warning glance as well. Yola knew better than to turn to see if Sindu was watching. She hung her head and allowed her crutches to drag in the dust like the wings of a wounded bird.

'Heyee, Yola? Was she casting a spell on me?'

'No, you are safe for now Shimima, but you will be turned into a toad if you make me laugh,' said Yola, keeping her head down. 'I'm in disgrace. Let's go.'

Shimima adjusted the ring of cloth on her head and swung the empty pot into place while Yola led the way, still dragging her crutches. They turned a bend in the path and Yola asked, her voice still subdued, 'Shimima, you turn and look, are we out of sight of home?'

Shimima turned gracefully under her pot. 'Yes, but wha ... Eyeee, careful Yola!'

Yola had thrown both crutches away and had both arms around her friend. 'If we're out of sight Shimima, I'm free, the spell is broken!'

But Shimima had both hands up, desperately holding on to her water pot. 'Yola, I may have two legs, but I have a pot on my head – whatever about your spell the pot must not be broken!' Yola hopped back while Shimima got control of her pot and rested it gently on the ground. 'It belonged to my husband's grandmother. Imagine if I dropped it!'

'Oh, Shimima, I have so much to say. Let's find somewhere to talk.'

They found a clearing in the bush a little off the path. Here the two girls talked and talked, sometimes seriously, sometimes laughing with their foreheads pressed together. In the end, Shimima knew all about Yola's trial, about Mr Hans – how lovely he was – and how Yola was going away, although she did not know how soon. Then Yola listened. She heard about Shimima's household and about Kimba, her funny husband, and the jokes he played. She thought she would like a funny husband. She imagined Shimima's house, laughing at the fun and goings-on inside. Shimima also told her secret things about marriage, things that Yola wanted to know.

Finally, they fell silent.

'I will miss you, Shimima.'

'When you come back you will have two legs again. You will walk down and see us, and if Kimba pulls your leg then it won't matter.'

Yola smiled at Shimima and didn't want to leave. Then Shimima said, 'Things will go along here, Yola. The sun will shine, I will carry the town's water supply on my head; a year is not a long time. I will think of you when the rains come again and will start then to look forward to the return of my little friend.'

6

The Road to Simbada

Yola felt she had hardly slept when Mother shook her awake. She sat on the edge of her bed, shivering slightly in the chill air before dawn. It was still pitch dark. A tiny yellow flame wobbled above the oil lamp on the table. She wasn't at all sure that she wanted to go now. She'd wanted Gabbin to see her off, but Senior Mother said no, no one must know when she was going. Now she was having difficulty getting her shoe on – either her foot had grown since her accident or it had just spread from walking barefoot. Mother helped her, speaking in whispers. A torch flashed in the doorway. Yola couldn't see who carried it, but recognised Senior Mother by her breathing, a strong inward breath followed by a gentle exhalation; you could tell a lot from Senior Mother's breathing. She played her torch over Yola, who was standing now, self-consciously, in a borrowed dress that Mother had let down so that it covered her stump. Senior Mother's hand appeared in the beam of the torch, holding an envelope; Mother took it.

'She is to get nothing that is not necessary, tell that to Mr Eriksen. She needs warm clothes, it will be cold even in summertime in Ireland. What is left will be her pocket money while she is in hospital. At school she will need less.'

'A girl from the office will take her shopping,' Mother explained.

Senior Mother sniffed significantly. 'Girls can be foolish together,' she said. 'Nothing unnecessary! Take the torch for the road and go quietly.' Senior Mother turned to Yola. 'A great loss, and now a great gain. Grow with it, but do not swell. May your ancestors watch over you.' She gave Yola a peck on the cheek and was gone.

Senior Mother had insisted that the Landcruiser was not to come up to the compound. There was to be no excitement; Yola was still in disgrace. Once they were outside the compound, Mother shone the torch on the road; snakes travel at night. It was pitch dark, there was not even a glimmer of light in the east: morning was a good hour off. Yola was sure they were too early but the Landcruiser was there, its headlights off, with just the dim glow of the little light over the windscreen. Hans was sitting in the passenger seat beside the driver, reading some papers. The back seat of the car seemed to be full of Kasemban deminers and the rear was piled high with bags and equipment. Yola wondered where she would sit. At that moment, Hans saw the torch and climbed out to shake hands with Mother.

'Good, Yola, you are on time, let's go. It is an eight-hour drive to Simbada. Have you ever been to the capital?' Yola said no. 'Let's get going!' he said.

Yola's goodbyes to Mother had to be hasty.

✦ ✧ ✦

The first hour of the drive was silent apart from the roar of the engine. They all felt tired after their early start. The Landcruiser threaded its way around the potholes as the road climbed up out of the Ruri river valley. The road had been smashed to bits during the war as both sides fought for possession of the Nopani

Bridge and the main road into the neighbouring country, Murabende, to the north. The headlights swung back and forth, illuminating outcrops of red rock at one moment, towering forest trees the next, or pocket-handkerchief plantations of bananas, where the green banana bunches ended in pendulous purple flowers. Morning mist clung low to the few fields that sloped up the valley sides. Yola felt sleepy and curiously content. She was sealed in a metal capsule, the forest out there was dark and mysterious, but sandwiched between Hans and the driver she felt safe and protected. She liked Hans, she liked him very much, she decided.

She realised she must have nodded off because, next thing, the cab was full of grey light, the forest had sunk back into the valley and they had emerged onto high ground, where the tawny grasses beside the road glowed briefly in the waning headlights. The acacia trees stood, waist high, ghostly in the mist. What happened next came as a complete surprise.

The car nosed down as the road dipped into a hollow. The driver swore. An impenetrable sea of mist rose outside the windows like muddy water. The driver was braking hard; the car slewed, but did not slow appreciably. Yola was holding her breath.

'Bad place!' he muttered. 'They put oil on the road!'

'Who?' she asked, but he did not answer. He was leaning forward, peering intently through the windscreen. He sucked in his breath. A man loomed out of the mist on the road ahead. Afterwards, Yola would remember him quite clearly. He had a filthy bush-hat pulled down over his face, two bandoleers of ammunition criss-crossed over his chest and in his hands was a sub-machine gun; it was raised towards them. Then something else caught Yola's eye: there was a log across the road. She shouted, but David, the driver had seen it too.

'Jump, Bandit!' he yelled, wrenching the wheel not away from the man but directly towards him. Yola saw the man's astonished face as he jumped clear, the wheels hit the end of the log and for an agonising moment Yola thought the car would turn over into the ditch, but then, screaming like a wounded elephant, it clawed back onto the road and accelerated up the hill and out of the mist. The men, startled into bleary wakefulness, started shouting and laughing and slapping the driver's back.

'Jump, Bandit, jump!' the men were shouting.

Yola looked around at Hans, who was smiling grimly at the excitement. Then one of the men started to sing a popular Kasembi song about a lover who had all sorts of problems with his girl, but he substituted the word 'bandit' for 'lover'. The result was hilarious and Yola joined in, hoping Hans didn't understand all the words.

They were clear of the fog pockets now and they stopped because the men wanted to get out. Yola noticed they did not leave the road, but stood at its edge; she turned her back. Hans came up after a little and offered her a bread roll.

'It is safer not to step off the tarmac, there are still landmines along the road edges. If you want to "go", I'll make the men look away,' he said.

'Why mine the edges?'

'In that way you force the enemy to walk on the road, then you can see them coming.'

'But that's where we, the women, walk – beside the tarmac, otherwise we get run over!'

'Soldiers don't think of women, just their own skins. They don't even think of the people they are supposed to be fighting for, just themselves.'

'Like the bandit? He had a gun.'

'Ya ya! Russia, America, Britain, China, they all sold guns to one side or the other. The government here is socialist, so they tried to nationalise your oil and minerals; the Americans and the British didn't like it. They had interests in these industries so they turned a blind eye when their arms dealers sold guns to the rebels – the Kasemba Liberation Army, the KLA. Then the Russians sold guns to the Kasemba government. But really what they all wanted was African oil and African copper ore, and to sell more guns so that they could make bigger and better guns to sell to the Arabs.'

'But the war is over. The KLA are defeated now, even my Uncle Banda, who was with the KLA, has handed in his Kalashnikov.'

'Ya, Yola my dear, but for how long? Just till someone sells him another one!'

'It's confusing.'

'It's criminal!' Hans snapped, his voice rising. 'What sickens me is that in some pretty house in America or Russia, the man who made that bandit's gun will have his morning coffee without a thought that Yola Abonda was nearly killed by one of his guns just now. It just makes me so angry!'

Yola stared at Hans. She had never before thought of how those faraway places could play a part in her own life. Should she be angry, like Hans?

'Come on, back on board!'

They were all wide awake now. The sun, which had shone briefly over the mist, now appeared as a glowing ball, sucking the fog up in a sheet. Underneath, the landscape appeared clean and fresh. David, the driver, thrust a tape into the tape deck on the dashboard, and music blared out. Hans yelled into Yola's ear that the volume button had fallen off so they couldn't turn it down; Yola didn't mind. The driver put his foot down and the road began to disappear under them faster and faster in a dizzy stream. Visibility was good now and they seemed to be skimming all but the largest potholes. Hans, seeing that her balance was not good without a second foot to brace herself with, laid his arm at the back of her seat, from time to time he steadied her with a hand on the shoulder; she was glad to have the road ahead to concentrate on. She closed her eyes against the giddy stream of the road. The music was from Zaire; voices rising on a magic carpet of heady rhythms.

Hans shouted in her ear, 'I used to think Latin American music came from America, but it is pure Africa. Just listen to that! When your people were taken away as slaves, they brought their music with them to America and gave rise to a whole new musical culture.'

Yola turned to tell Hans how it made her want to dance, but at that moment the two-way radio, which was bolted to the dashboard, gave a series of hisses and pops.

'It's time for a radio check,' Hans shouted.

She watched, fascinated, as he leaned forward and took the microphone from the dashboard. David switched off the tape and Hans took up a microphone and started calling.

'One-five bravo calling Simbada. One-five bravo calling Simbada. Come in, please.'

The radio hissed back at him. He twirled a knob, head cocked to one side, listening. Suddenly the hissing stopped and a voice cut in.

'... avo, do you read me?'

'One-five bravo, receiving you Simbada.'

'Carry on one-five. That's Hans, isn't it?'

'Ya, ya, Hans here.'

Every hour, as they drove, Hans radioed to the NPA head office in Simbada, telling them how far they had got and how they were faring. The bandit was reported so that other cars could be warned.

◆　◇　◆

Yola couldn't believe that it was still only midday when they drove down into Simbada. She had never been in Simbada before – the civil war had meant that no one travelled unless it was absolutely necessary, and then only with an escort of soldiers. She was a little disappointed; it was very like Nopani, acres of mud-brick houses with corrugated iron roofs. The roads between the houses were mud roads, but unlike Nopani, heaps of rubbish were piled wherever there was a space. Children crawled over these like maggots.

'Hans,' she asked in disgust, 'why is there rubbish everywhere?'

'Because the city councillor who is responsible for clearing the streets is corrupt,' Hans replied. 'He has a big Mercedes and a luxury house in the hills. He gives all the street-cleaning contracts to his friends for big bribes. They then buy smaller Mercedes with the money the government gives them, but they don't do the work.'

'But in Nopani the streets are clean, why?'

'They are clean because a certain Chief Abonda is not corrupt and sees that the money is spent on brushes and brooms.'

'Abonda? Father? Father has no Mercedes. He has no car. We have electricity only in the main house. He can't be such a great man!'

'Yola, child, you are as bad as the rest of them. Your father is a greater man than half the government here in Simbada put together.'

Yola thought about this. Father had always just been the chief and did the things chiefs do. He had an office in Nopani and he walked the two miles to it every day, otherwise people came to him. It had never occurred to her to think that he was special. She looked at the rubbish outside the window and suddenly changed her mind. Yes, Father was special. Quite vividly she remembered the time he had entered into her mind at her trial; that was special. She turned to tell Hans, but stopped. Some instinct told her that Hans might not understand. There were things about Africa that she knew but that he did not. She smiled to herself; she must look after Hans.

The rebels had never captured Simbada, so the wide colonial streets of the city centre with their gardened mansions still stood in shabby glory; in Nopani, the houses were like eyeless corpses. Here they were intact and the walls were not pock-marked with bullet holes and shrapnel. She gazed in wonder at the blaze of flowers on the bushes that divided the traffic on the road. They passed some government buildings with their flags flying, and smart, clean soldiers on guard. There seemed to be soldiers everywhere – some slouching in alleyways, some sitting, bored, in the backs of trucks. The Landcruiser turned off the main road and pulled up outside a low building. A tree with purple flowers wept tresses over the gate. Yola recognised the sign and logo: Northern People's Aid. They had arrived.

7

Isabella

The heat, which had been kept at bay while the car was moving, hit them like a wall when the car doors were opened. Hans was preoccupied, putting his papers into his briefcase. Yola suddenly felt alone, abandoned. He jumped down and seemed to be about to dash off, when he remembered her and turned to help her down; her crutches were passed out over the men's heads.

'I must find Isabella for you,' he said. Yola remembered that Isabella was 'the girl from the office'. 'The meeting has started, so I must be quick. You will like Isabella, she is from Angola. She was born Senhora Isabella Alvares, how about that for a name? She will take you to the shops and the market, she knows what you will need. We all speak English here by the way, even if our accents are a little strange!'

As they walked down the cool corridors, Yola could hear a voice talking on the radio – the other end of the conversations she had heard in the car. On her right a door stood half-open. She had a momentary glimpse of a shiny table, an orderly scatter of papers on it, and of faces – white and black – turned towards an unseen speaker. One chair was empty, that must be Hans's. He opened a door at the end of the corridor leading to an office. Hans blundered about looking for a chair for her to sit on. A door at the opposite end of the room opened and a woman hurried in carrying a sheaf of papers.

'Sorry I'm late, Hans,' she began, then she saw Yola and smiled saying, 'Yola? That's right, isn't it?'

Yola stared at her open-mouthed. She had expected a European, but this woman was African, vibrant and sophisticated at the same time. She was dressed very simply in tight blue jeans and a black halter-neck top. She was the most beautiful woman Yola had ever seen! Yola was captivated. Without thinking she breathed out, 'You are beautiful!' and then immediately wished she hadn't. But the woman just threw her head back and laughed.

'Hans!' she exclaimed, waving him away, 'you better go out while Yola and I admire each other!'

He closed the door as he left. The woman came over, kissed Yola quickly on the cheek and said, 'I'm sorry I am late, but I forgot that the Embassy would be closed over lunch. Anyhow, we've got all your papers sorted out, we just have to get them all in order, then the next thing will be to do some shopping. Coffee?'

It was when Isabella said 'coffee' that Yola realised her voice had the added charm of an accent. Hans had said that she came from Angola. Of course, she would speak Portuguese.

◆　◇　◆

The desk seemed to be covered with papers, all to do with Yola's impending exile. She had had no idea that it would take this much work. There was a passport, a visa for Ireland and there were medical reports from the hospital about her amputation. She began to feel uneasy – how would she manage in Ireland on her own? Her stump began to hurt, throbbing and burning from the battering it had got in the car. She had a sudden guilty feeling when she found herself thinking, I don't need a new leg, I'm getting on fine on crutches. I didn't want anyone messing with me!

'Why … why are you doing all this for me?' she asked in a small voice. Isabella leant back and looked at her, head on one side, serious for a moment.

'Yola, my friend, don't ask. We do it because we want to, like your Sister Martha wants to, like your father wants to. You see, Hans has told me all about you. If you ask too much "why", either you will get cocky – I think you can be cocky, yes?' Yola smiled. 'Or you will start to feel guilty. You will get a new leg, you will learn a little at school; that's all we want. You can decide yourself then what you do with your life.'

'But who … why?' wondered Yola.

Isabella laughed. 'Too many questions, Yola.' She swept the papers together. 'That's enough philosophy. Come on, let's go shopping.'

Yola was happy again.

◆   ◇   ◆

Isabella took Yola into town in her battered little green car.

'I'm afraid it is rather old,' she said.

It looked so fragile and unthreatening after the Landcruiser that Yola laughed in delight. They left it under the guard of a Gabbin-like urchin with half a tip, the other half to be tendered when they got back.

Isabella seemed to have an instinct for what clothes Yola would need, and where to find them. Yola followed her in a happy daze. From time to time, Senior Mother's envelope would appear and money would be extracted. They laughed till it hurt in the fitting-room of Simbada's main department store as Yola tried on some of the more outrageous outfits.

Then Isabella took Yola down an alleyway and in through a

bead curtain into a tiny passage of a shop, where an old Indian tradesman greeted Isabella like his daughter. Amid the spicy smells of Indian cooking they looked at skirts that would keep an Eskimo warm. Isabella bargained and the old Indian almost wept, but when the time came for them to leave, the old man almost wept again and gave them small spicy cakes. They went to the market to look for a suitcase. The market seemed to stretch to the horizon and even Isabella had to ask where the suitcase stalls were. The man who sold them the case was also from Angola.

'Bom dia,' he greeted Isabella, smiling, and Yola listened entranced while they spoke together in Portuguese.

Late in the day, they sat under a tree outside a café at the edge of the market and sipped ice coffee. Isabella explained that Yola would have a travel companion as far as Brussels. His name was Knutt, he had malaria and was being sent home to Norway to rest. Yola relaxed, she was exhausted but happy. There was a lull in their conversation. For a moment, the whole day was condensed in Yola's mind. Behind it all was Hans – Hans who had started all this for her and opened up a life she thought closed forever, Hans who had encouraged her, and Hans who she had so enjoyed being close to on the road from Nopani. Without thinking she said, 'I like Hans.'

Isabella looked at her, her head cocked to one side and one eyebrow raised, then she said, 'So do I. But then, he's my husband.'

8

Into Exile

Yola was really embarrassed that she had cried in front of Isabella the night before. She had been so tired. The more she had tried to explain her tears, the more embarrassing and ridiculous it had become. It must be so obvious that she had got too fond of Hans. She had slept the night on a settee in their sitting-room and she thought she could hear them talking about her. In the morning, Hans seemed a little restrained, while Isabella was as nice as ever.

Both of them came to see her off at the airport. Knutt, who was accompanying Yola as far as Brussels, had already gone through the boarding gate. It was time to say goodbye. Yola had planned a kiss for Isabella and a handshake for Hans. As she turned to them she could see that they were embarrassed for her. All her gratitude flooded back, but she could not ... no, must not get emotional again. A thought came to her; she turned to Hans with an impish smile and said, 'Hans, I'm so glad you have such a beautiful wife!'

She had never seen Hans startled before. 'Ya, ya. But why?'

'Because otherwise I would have to marry you myself, and you are far too old!'

She picked up her hand luggage and fled. No kisses. She

turned just before passing into the departure area. Hans and Isabella had their arms around each other and were laughing and waving.

✦ ✧ ✦

The airhostess had wanted to put Yola in the aisle seat, where it would be easier for her to get in and out. But Yola had looked so disappointed that she had relented and let her shuffle her way in to the window seat, where she sat, waiting for her heart to stop racing. How did the other passengers manage to look so calm? It wasn't just the sights that were new to her, it was everything; she found her nose twitching like a rabbit's at new scents and smells. A white woman had sat beside her in the departure lounge, wafting a soft but invisible cloud of perfume about her. Yola was intrigued, but strangely disturbed. Masked by the fragrance of the perfume she recognised something animal, the scent of the civet cat perhaps, but infinitely refined. Was there a feline animal underneath the woman's flowery fragrance? She shuddered slightly; the fear of the cat is an ancient one. (Once, when she and Shimima were walking home in the dark, they had seen green eyes in the beam of their torch and had heard the panting grunt of a leopard. But strong, sensible Shimima wouldn't let Yola run and they got home safely.)

Knutt, his skin yellow from the quinine he was taking for his malaria, was sitting beside her. He searched in the pocket on the back of the seat in front and pulled out a glossy flight magazine.

'There'll be one in your pouch, too,' he said.

Yola nodded. Any other time she would have pounced on a magazine, but just now there was too much to see. She heard a thump, peered out of the window and saw the steps that they had just climbed up being drawn away. This was the moment. There was no turning back now.

The aircraft stood at the end of the runway shuddering, the

roar of the engines mounted. Yola dug her nails deep into her palms as their thunder grew and grew. The pilot released the brakes and the unexpected surge of acceleration pressed her back into her seat. She struggled against it, fighting against the surge and – if she had known it – fighting against her exile. The nose of the aircraft lifted and the plane began to climb. Yola turned to look out of the window, pressing her forehead against it and straining to look down. The plane banked and she was looking into a compound, very like her own at home; she could see that people had stopped what they were doing to look up at the plane above them. She closed her eyes, wanting to preserve this little piece of Africa and take it with her. When she came back those people would come to life again: the woman would pick up the water jar she had put down to watch the plane; the boy would scuttle off to stop his goats from eating the thatch on the huts. She held on to the picture, but the golden thread that was holding her to home was stretching ... stretching; fearful that it might break, she let go.

They climbed on and on through grey haze. Then, just as Yola was thinking of sitting back, the haze sank below them and the world appeared. She gasped – there was the curving horizon, while above it the sky arched up, blue as a bird's wing, darkening almost to black directly overhead. She gazed at the horizon again and the great globe of the earth seemed to spin beneath her. Africa would wait for her; she was on her great adventure, and everything was new.

When her neck was tired from craning out, she sank back into her seat and stole a glance at Knutt. His eyes were closed and his skin was lightly beaded with sweat. He needed a spell in Norway to recover. He was one of the dog-trainers who taught dogs to locate landmines buried in the ground. In Brussels, he would see her on to her flight to Dublin. She wanted to ask him about his work, but he seemed to be asleep already. She decided that he was dreaming of fjords and withdrew into her own thoughts.

◆　◇　◆

Yola nearly had a fight with Knutt in Brussels airport.

'I won't take a wheelchair! I'm not a cripple. It's just I only have one leg!'

'But please Yola, we have been flying all night, you might fall asleep. Once you are in the wheelchair, I will know that they will look after you and see that you get your flight.'

An announcer said something in an incomprehensible language and Knutt broke off, head on one side, listening.

'Look, Yola, they are calling my flight. Please?' he begged. Poor Knutt, he looked so sick and yellow.

'All right, but promise me that when I come home you will teach me how to look for mines with a dog.' Knutt, who would have promised Yola anything at this stage, relaxed.

'Ya ya, sure Yola, sure.'

'In that case,' she said grandly, 'I will sit in this chair thing and release you to go back to the fjord you were dreaming about.' She stretched up and kissed him on the cheek.

As she was wheeled off she had to laugh. Knutt, who'd hardly said a word the whole trip, was rubbing his cheek where she had kissed him. But whether he was more surprised at the kiss or at her knowing that he'd been dreaming about fjords, she couldn't say.

◆　◇　◆

'Ladies and gentlemen, please fasten your seatbelts. We are on our final approach to Dublin airport, where we will be landing in approximately five minutes.'

Yola, head turned to the window as usual, strained to look down. Below, little blue waves glistened in the sun, and the occasional white-top showed bright and then faded as the wave moved on. A ship trailed a creamy wake behind it. An island appeared, rising ruggedly out of the sea, and white specks – birds, perhaps – wheeled against its dark cliffs. There was a group of white-painted houses, a toy harbour and then the sea racing below, browning towards the approaching land.

'It really *is* green!' she murmured to herself.

She turned back from the window only when the passengers started to struggle to their feet and open the overhead lockers. A middle-aged woman sitting beside her smiled.

'God bless you child, I thought you would put your head out through that window before we were landed. Are you coming to Ireland on holiday?'

'It feels like a holiday,' Yola explained, 'but I'm really coming for a new leg. Then I'll go to school for a whole year.'

Yola moved slightly and the woman looked down.

'A new leg? God save us and I never noticed! Oh dear.' She went on saying 'Oh dear' as she pulled down her handbag. Then, as if she'd forgotten something, she opened her bag and rummaged. She reached across and pressed something into Yola's hand. 'I'm sure he's sorry he's late, but he will help you on your travels, dear.'

Then she was gone, still fluttering anxiously. Yola opened her hand and there was a worn, but well polished, white metal medal of a saint, a child on his shoulder and waves about his feet.

Yola hoped she'd see the little woman again to thank her, but she didn't. She was wheeled out by side passages and concrete tunnels to the baggage-reclaim area. When they emerged, her case was circulating on the carousel alone and her immediate anxiety now was whether or not there would be anyone to meet her.

9

Catherine

A nun, just like Sister Martha but much younger and dressed in a neat suit, had met her at the airport. She introduced herself as Sister Attracta. She had a funny sing-song accent. She said she was from Cork so proudly that Yola didn't like to ask where Cork was. Yola was amazed to find the car parked on the roof of the airport. Sister Attracta wanted to hear all about her flight and how she had managed in Brussels. Yola told her of her confrontation with Knutt and she laughed.

'Poor boy, he probably felt pretty awful if he'd had malaria,' she said. The traffic was getting thicker and she changed the subject. 'We wanted to bring you to our house here in Dublin Yola, so you could rest, but it is getting close to the beginning of term and it would be nice to get you fixed up with your new leg before the autumn term starts. I hope that is all right; I'll be taking you straight to the clinic. They are expecting you there.'

A huge articulated lorry crowded them against the pavement and Sister Attracta leaned on the horn. Yola noticed her lips moving as they ground to a halt at the curb.

'Ought I confess what I *nearly* said?' she said with a sheepish grin. But Yola didn't smile, she was beginning to panic.

'So many people, so many cars!' she said as a flow of office girls and young men in suits and jackets surrounded them. She wanted to shrink. The journey and the new sights were beginning to tell. Her stump felt hot, which was often a prelude to it hurting. All these confident young people who knew where they were going intimidated her.

'You must be dying to get rid of those old crutches,' said Sister Attracta. For no reason that Yola could think of, tears started flooding into her eyes. She liked her crutches, they were part of her and of home. Uncle Banda had made them for her. She didn't want anyone messing around with her leg; it was throbbing and sore. She wanted to see the sea again and then go home exactly as she was. They crossed a bridge; they must be near a harbour because there were ships. She turned to stare at them. Perhaps one of them was going to Africa. Homesickness flooded over her. Sister Attracta paid money at a kiosk while Yola managed a surreptitious wipe of her face.

◆　◇　◆

When they had arrived at the clinic, Yola was walked for miles down corridors, crutches slipping on polished floors. Finally, they had turned into a bright, clean ward with four empty beds that looked so comfortable, Yola would gladly have climbed in, clothes and all. A nurse helped her undress and then pulled the curtains around her bed, but Yola was already asleep.

◆　◇　◆

She was woken by someone peering at her between the curtains. It was a girl, but she was so fair and fuzzy that Yola found herself blinking at her in disbelief.

'Oh, hello. Are you awake?'

She was younger than Yola, but it was difficult for Yola to tell how old Europeans were. The girl slipped in through the curtains.

'I'm Catherine. I can't shake hands because I don't have my arms on. I was in physio when you arrived. You must have been tired. I've looked in on you a couple of times and you were asleep. Wasn't I good not to wake you? It gets boring in here sometimes.' She plonked down on the edge of Yola's bed. 'You don't mind, do you. Sister gets furious when I sit on people's beds. There's three of us in here, and now you. Susan's only little. She's got callipers 'cos her leg's all shrunk. Then there's Brigid the Hump. Lots of trauma – car accident – lost a foot, I think; she spends a lot of time with the shrink.'

'Sorry,' interrupted Yola, hitching herself up in the bed, hoping to slow the flow of talk, 'what is a shrink?'

An anxious look crossed the girl's face; she was very pretty. 'Sorry, me speak quickly. You speak English? You African?' Yola had to laugh.

'Yes I speak English, but there are words I don't understand like, well, shrink?'

Her new friend looked relieved and patted Yola reassuringly on the knee. 'Oh good, I'd die if I couldn't talk to you. A shrink is a psychiatrist or psy ... something, at any rate poor Brigid's head's all messed up after her accident. Trauma, like I said. That's why I call her The Hump – not to her face, of course. When she sees me coming she pretends she's asleep and hunches up. I know when I'm not wanted. I wouldn't know about trauma, see, I'm congenital – born like this.'

She waved her arms in front of Yola, only the vestiges of fingers remained on the shortened forearms. Yola felt sorry for her, but felt more than a pang of sympathy for poor Brigid. She didn't understand half of what the girl was saying, but decided it was easier to let the flow of talk run on. Anyway, she was fascinated by the girl's bright, bright blue eyes. Catherine seemed to know all about the clinic and what was going to happen to Yola.

'They'll measure you up tomorrow. You're an above-the-knee amputation, aren't you?' Yola nodded. 'See! I told you so,

I could tell from the blankets. Then they'll X-ray you. You might need surgery,' she said with relish. 'The physiotherapists are the ones that knock you about, Pummel and Poke we call them. They will give you all sorts of exercises to do. It's fun really. They wear blue; the occupational therapists are the ones in green. I was told they'd try to make me knit or weave baskets, but it's sensibler things like learning to tie your shoelaces.

'Let me see, what next? Oh yes, next they will make a cast of your stump. That's fun. There's this cute boy working in the labs. I fancy him. He's learning. They are working on my new arm at this very moment. It will look great. Oh hell!' she exclaimed suddenly. 'You know what? I can't catch you out now! Pity, 'cos what I really like is shaking hands with someone new and watching their face! It's really gas when they suddenly feel this dead thing in their hand. You see them longing to drop it – *Yuck!* – but then they realise that would be rude, so they begin to shake it, not a normal shake but like they were shaking a dog's paw. It will be great though, with my new hand I will be able to grip them like Frankenstein. Come to meet thy doom,' she intoned in a sepulchral voice. At that moment there was a clatter at the door. 'Great! The shop trolley – want anything? – see you,' and she was gone.

Feeling slightly battered, Yola lay back and digested what Catherine had said. It was all so nice here. She thought of the rough and ready conditions at the hospital in Nopani. Through the gap in the curtains left by Catherine's sudden exit, she could see a vase of yellow flowers on the windowsill. The only place she'd seen flowers in a vase before had been in a magazine. For all Catherine's gruesome delight, Yola wasn't frightened, not even of surgery. Her tears in the car yesterday seemed ridiculous now. She had come all this way to get a new leg. Of course she wanted it!

It all happened much as Catherine had outlined. The X-rays of Yola's leg were excellent, there were no 'spurs', as they called them, growing on the bone, which meant she wouldn't need another operation. The doctor was full of praise for her surgeon in Nopani, especially when he heard about the power cut during the operation. A technician in a white coat, called Mr Dwyer, explained how they would cover her stump with cling film before making the cast. Yola had never heard of cling film, so he showed her a roll. Then they would cover this over with a thick layer of plaster of Paris, a sort of cement that would set in a few minutes. It might get a little warm as it set, but that was all. Then they would slide the plaster shell off and make a soft plastic socket for her stump from that.

Catherine was waiting for her at the door as she set out for the fitting-room.

'Goodbye Yola, be brave, it's been nice knowing you.' She flicked a mock tear from her eye. 'My hand in friendship before you depart.'

Yola, who had grown very fond of the child, put out her hand without thinking. Her yip of surprise echoed down the corridor. It was bad enough when she gripped this dead-but-alive thing Catherine offered, but when it began to tighten around her own hand it was just too much. A nurse looked out to see what was going on and shouted at the otherwise delighted Catherine.

'Catherine Maloney, if you scare one more person with that hand of yours I'll have it off you!'

Yola was still smiling when she got to the fitting-room. So that was Catherine's Frankenstein grip!

Mr Dwyer, the technician, kept up an easy flow of conversation as he worked, covering her stump with cling film. She hardly noticed the boy who was working nearby, mixing something, plaster of Paris she presumed, in a plastic bucket. She was still smiling to herself, thinking about Catherine, when she looked up and found him looking at her. It was rather like her first meeting with Hans – she hadn't meant to smile at Hans either. The boy smiled back, but then looked away.

She looked down at her leg. It glistened ultra black under the cling film. A memory, vaguely disturbing, was forming in her mind; a smell, familiar but frightening, was teasing her nostrils. Apprehension pricked: what did her leg remind her of? Then she had it – it was that time when Hans had taken Gabbin and her up to see the demining on the hill. Hans had opened a mine like the one that had wounded her and it had lain in his hand like an oyster. She felt panic growing in her like a sneeze, it was rising ... rising. She tried to hold her breath against the cinnamon scent. A bell was ringing down the corridor – Managu's, perhaps? Mr Dwyer moulded the first dollop of plaster about her leg. Then suddenly she knew! That was not her leg, it was a detonator, black and shiny, and the white stuff was the explosive.

'Hans! Gabbin! Get away! Don't press the trigger! Don't press it! It will go off ...'

The scent of cinnamon exploded in her nostrils and she was screaming. Her head was pressed against the white coat of Mr Dwyer, who was holding her and shouting to the boy to strip the plaster and the cling film from her leg. People were running. The whole hospital seemed to be focussed on her. Yola screamed and screamed. Suddenly she wanted these nice complaisant people to know what it was like to suffer. She lifted her head and filled her lungs – she was enjoying herself, but then she was aware of someone watching her, someone who knew what she was doing. The boy had staggered back, his hands white, cling film hanging in streamers, and she was staring into his eyes. Something in the boy's expression reminded her of Father. She opened her mouth to scream again, but the power seemed to have gone from her lungs. Against her will she saw herself as the boy was seeing her – a small girl looking for attention – and her scream died to a sob; she dropped her head.

Mr Dwyer moved back; concerned hands helped Yola to stand. A rainbow of coloured uniforms had swirled to her aid. She heard Mr Dwyer saying, 'Don't worry, there's no hurry. We'll try again some other time.'

Then he turned to the boy. 'Fintan, we'd better get this cleaned up before it begins to set.'

Yola couldn't look up.

That evening Fintan wrote in his diary:

A strange thing happened today. There's this little African girl, Yola somebody, who threw a wobbly when we were trying to make her cast. I had to take the plaster and cling film off her stump – quickly. All the while she was going at it some. Lots of noise, everyone rushing to help. I got the cling film off and was standing back dripping plaster when – strange – even though she was still going at it hammer and tongs, something told me that the crisis had passed. She looked up at me then, taking in air for the next blast. Without thinking, I gave her our old science teacher's 'sceptical eyebrow'. I don't know how, but that did it; she collapsed in a heap, genuine tears, fit over. Cured. For about half a minute I felt really pleased with myself – I'd snapped her out of it. Now I feel such a fraud. Who am I to stop that kid yelling out in protest – and that's what it was. While Dwyer was working, her good leg was stretched out beside him, beautiful, like a young athlete's, and some bastard has to blow the other one off down to an obscene stump.

10

Fintan

'*You lucky thing!* Fintan to show you around, oh passion!'
Catherine struck her chest and sighed theatrically.
'Patients are not allowed in the labs, you know – at least *I'm*
not! How did you manage it? He's gorgeous!'

'I didn't *manage* it. I just got a bit upset when they tried to
make my cast; they think it may help if I can see how they make
them – casts and legs and things.'

Yola was nervous of another attack and she was also apprehensive about the boy. She felt he'd seen a side of her that she
would have liked to conceal. She had been enjoying having
everyone rush to her aid; then she'd noticed him looking at her
as if he could see through her – see that the fuss she was making
was no longer genuine. She groaned inwardly. It was bad
enough having a father who could mind-read you! She tried to
picture the boy. He was shorter and darker than Hans, and he
had dark, penetrating eyes. His smile before her panic attack
had been nice.

'Look Catherine, please. I want to think.'

'Thinking's bad for you. I never think,' said Catherine with
genuine concern.

At that moment there was a knock on the door. Yola saw

the flash of a white lab-coat.

'Oh *do* come in,' called Catherine. 'Sadly, we're quite decent.'

'It's Miss Abonda I'm looking for.'

Yola realised she wasn't going to have time to think. This must be Fintan now. Catherine swooned convincingly, but it was wasted – Fintan didn't come in to the room.

Yola had been given new elbow crutches with rubber caps that didn't slip but squeaked on the polished floor. The boy didn't look up when she came out, he turned to lead the way down the corridor. Yola followed him warily, keeping to the opposite side of the corridor. They came to a pair of swing doors. He opened them for her, giving the far door a flick so that she could get through before it swung to behind her. He still hadn't met her eye.

They entered a large laboratory. While Yola looked around, Fintan went off to find his boss. Workbenches divided up the room. Feet and legs stuck up in the air from the benches, as if their owners were taking a nap somewhere underneath. A hand rose from a bench and clutched at the air while its owner drowned somewhere among the paint pots and brushes below. A man was working at one bench. He had turned back the stocking sheath on a leg and was working with a screwdriver on a complicated joint, which Yola realised must be a knee. He looked up and winked at her. Then Fintan came back.

'Mr Dwyer says he is sorry but he is very busy so he can't join us. He's asked me to show you around. Do you mind?'

'No, I'd like to see ... well, everything.'

'Not ... bothered anymore?' he asked tentatively.

'No, I think not. Sorry, I ...' she wasn't sure how to finish.

'I thought it was great.' He smiled for the first time. 'Come on, let's talk to Sam. He's our paint and colour expert.'

For the next hour they moved through the lab. Yola felt relaxed, like she did with Hans. The technicians were delighted to show her what they were doing. Sam, in particular, was pleased.

'I'm sick of pink!' he exclaimed. 'Show me your hands, dear. Beautiful! Fintan, just look at those, stroke them! Pure mahogany.'

Fintan went pink; he was good at explaining the workings of the lab to her though. She saw how the metal joints worked and how these were sheathed in carefully moulded and painted plastic so that the limbs looked indistinguishable from the real thing.

'We'll cross over to the casting room now,' Fintan said when they had finished in the main lab. 'It is rather noisy in there; the pumps are running.'

In the casting room, a white-coated man was sanding down what was obviously the plaster cast of a stump; a second was peering into an oven. Fintan flicked the lights on and off and they turned to see who had come in. He mouthed something to them and they both responded with smiles and thumbs-up signs.

'The men in here,' he shouted, 'are deaf, so the noise of the vacuum pumps doesn't bother them. But don't think that they can't understand what you're saying. They can lip-read at a hundred metres!' The man at the stump grinned and wagged a finger at Fintan. 'See what I mean!' he laughed and mouthed something to the man at the oven, who raised three fingers in response.

'Three minutes and the plastic will be ready,' Fintan shouted to Yola. Then the man looked at Fintan and, with a grin, tapped his jacket and imitated someone playing a flute. Fintan shouted in Yola's ear, 'Watch this!' He fished in his coat and pulled out a tiny little flute and held it sideways to his lips. He nodded to the technician, tapped with his foot one, two, three, and started to play. Yola leaned close to him, so that she could hear, then to her amazement the technician, who was a big man, suddenly began to dance. She couldn't believe it; the man was dancing in perfect time to Fintan's playing, despite the noise. She had seen dancing like this on the television in the ward.

'Riverdance!' she shouted in delight.

Fintan nodded without stopping. The music went on, then, without any apparent signal between them, the dancer and flute stopped on the one note and Fintan and the white-coated technician bowed solemnly to each other.

'That's our party piece,' Fintan shouted as Yola applauded. 'Don't tell Mr Dwyer, but that's how we fill our day.' He pocketed his flute.

'But how–?' Yola started.

Fintan laughed. 'It's a secret! Look. He's about to make a socket. Come over.'

Yola let him take her arm and draw her over to the oven, from which the flushed technician was taking what looked like a small window frame. Beside him was the machine that was making all the noise; mounted on it was the plaster cast of somebody's stump. Instead of glass, the frame contained a sheet of hot plastic. Slowly and carefully he lowered this down over the stump so that it draped over it like a shroud.

'Now watch how the vacuum sucks it tight on to the cast!' Fintan said in Yola's ear.

Feeling almost as if it were closing about her own leg, she saw the plastic shrink and tighten to a perfect fit. She gave a little sigh and, for the first time, began to feel really comfortable with the idea of a new leg. It had been a good idea to come and see all this.

✦ ✧ ✦

The technicians were leaving for lunch, hanging their coats behind the door. They waved to Yola and Fintan and left. Fintan reached in behind the machine and flicked a switch. A welcome silence fell over them.

'So the whole thing's not too frightening, is it?' He lifted down a socket like the one they had just seen made, blew some dust off it and handed it to Yola.

'Go on, feel it, this is what you will actually have against your skin. See, it is quite soft and flexible. It will fit you like a glove. As you get stronger your muscles will be able to push this in and out as they work. We can also leave space in the casing that we put around this so that, if you lunge forward, it won't hurt. The leg is bolted on firmly, and then the whole socket is enclosed in an outer casing hand-painted by artist Sam.'

'Won't it fall off? How will I keep it on?' Yola asked.

'You'll be shown. First you will bandage your stump tightly – that will make it smaller and your leg will slip into the socket easily. You will pull the bandage off through this hole; your leg expands then, so that when you seal the hole the leg stays on by suction. Simple!' Yola looked sceptical. He laughed. 'We'll have you running in a few weeks if you really give it a try. But look at the time, sorry I've kept you so long.' He turned to put the socket back on to the shelf.

It came as a shock to Yola that this was the end. She would go back to her ward now, but there were things she still needed to ask him, like how the technician had danced without hearing, and … and, well, other things. She wanted to see him again, but she couldn't very well ask.

Fintan was unbuttoning his lab-coat when the doors swung open.

'Oh there you are!' It was Mr Dwyer. 'Sorry to have left you, but you were in good hands. Fintan, why don't you take Yola and go to the canteen? It's lunchtime.' He turned to Yola. 'Fintan's dad has a project in Africa, ask him about it. I will have half an hour at two o'clock and we can wind up then with any questions. All right?'

✦ ✧ ✦

They sat in a corner of the canteen within a protective shield of clattering cutlery and lunchtime chatter. Yola was too excited to eat. She was overwhelmed by the noise, the colours and by how everything shone and looked new. She thought about home, where everything was either homemade or mended. Fintan had put down his tray and was deftly organising his plate, knife, fork and spoon. Yola watched and imitated, but got everything reversed. What were they going to talk about? Fintan seemed tongue-tied too and had gone pink. She was amused by how Europeans went pink when they were embarrassed. Then, she knew what she would ask.

'Mr Fintan, how did he do it? The man in the lab, dancing. I could hardly hear your playing above the noise, and you say he's deaf?'

Fintan smiled and laughed. 'First, just call me Fintan. Second, if I tell you, you promise you won't tell.' Yola nodded, delighted. 'Well, his name is Sean – I'll spell that for you later – he's been deaf since he got measles as a baby. He has a twin sister – Mary, I think – who was big into Irish dancing. Sean would be taken to watch her. The teacher was a fiddler.' He mimed a fiddler playing and raised an eyebrow to see if Yola understood; she nodded. 'After a while, Sean noticed that while Mary was dancing, the teacher's foot was working up and down in time to the music. Suddenly he thought, I could dance too! All he had to do was to keep his eye on the teacher's foot and copy Mary's steps.

'They were a sensation together. People thought it was a miracle: a deaf boy dancing! They went in for competitions and won. Then, one day, a big competition came up. They waited and waited, but their teacher never turned up; his car had broken down. No problem, there was another fiddler who could play for them. They got up on the stage and Sean had his eye on the fiddler's foot. Suddenly he saw the bow moving and Mary taking off into the dance, but poor Sean could not move.'

'Why?'

'Because this new fiddler didn't tap his foot. So Sean had nothing to dance to. He told me: "The fiddler's feet might have been screwed to the floor, and so were mine!" So, that was the end of his dancing career.'

'So he was watching your foot tapping? He couldn't hear anything?'

Fintan nodded and Yola's laughter rang out. Heads turned in the canteen and people smiled.

'Tell me all about Ireland,' Yola said, with an expansive gesture. 'Are you going to be a player of the flute?'

To her surprise, Fintan's face darkened. Had she said the wrong thing? She noticed that his hand had drifted to the pocket where his flute was hidden, as if defending it. A gap was opening in the conversation. Then Fintan seemed to pull himself out of his dark mood.

'Sorry, it's just that the flute is a sore point at the moment.' Yola wondered what a sore point was but bit her lip. 'This is not a proper flute, just a baby one, a piccolo that will fit in my pocket. My real flute's ... well ... I haven't got a real flute anymore.'

He got up and brought them both a cup of coffee. Yola sensed he didn't want to talk about his flute or how he had lost it.

'Tell me about Ireland,' she asked, 'the place you come from. I know so little.'

'I live in a small town in the midlands of Ireland, it's called Caherisce,' he began.

'Green fields?' asked Yola wistfully.

'Lots and lots of green fields, and a brown mountain with goats and sheep on it. There are rocks on the mountain and a sturdy little river. My family were blacksmiths. Do you know what those are? People who work in metal, making horse-shoes and ploughs and things. Then Grandfather started a factory. He made spades and pickaxes, using the waterpower from the river to hammer and beat the metal. I would go down there as a kid; it was all noise, red metal and white sparks. O'Farrell Engineering it was then. Granddad would say, "Fifty sweaty workers, lad, and that means fifty pay pack-ets into fifty homes add fifty wives with fifty shopping bags ..." well, he'd go on and on. When my father took over, the business was already in trouble; no one wanted our spades or pickaxes any more. Dad looked around and saw how the plas-tics industry was growing, and changed the factory so that we were making things out of plastic instead of steel. To begin with it was great, people would come, explain what they wanted and Dad would design and make it. Then we found the snag. As soon as we had got the product perfect the cus-tomers said, "Sorry, we can get this made cheaper in Taiwan or Korea." The factory closed just before Christmas, and that's why I'm here.'

'Because you have no work?' asked Yola.

'Oh no, I'm still at school. This is a holiday job. I've been here all summer.' He sighed. 'You see, my dad thinks it will be good training for me because they work in plastics here.'

'But don't you like it here?' asked Yola, surprised.

'I like it here because Mr Dwyer's decent. I like the technicians; we have a lot of fun – Sean and his dancing. Then there are the patients, you and Catherine, but not *plastics*!' He said it with such vehemence that they both laughed.

'But why – why do you have to?' Yola thought of life in Africa, where everything seemed to be planned from birth: minding babies, grinding corn, getting married, more babies, work, work, work; while here it seemed that a person could do anything they liked.

'It's for my dad's sake, Yola. He walks about the house at night thinking how he's let Grandfather down and how half the town is out of work because of him. He curses and swears and he doesn't go out anymore. I think it's because he doesn't want to meet the men that used to work for us. I thought I'd be able to do my own thing this summer – the Youth Orchestra have a summer camp, I had a place – then, just before the holidays, this miracle man appeared with a huge contract in Africa that looks like putting Dad right back in business, and me, of course, right back in plastics.' A cloud crossed Fintan's face. 'Then Dad … it was an accident really …'

Yola wanted to ask, What accident? but didn't dare. His hand had crept back into his pocket where he kept his tiny flute. She so wanted to know, but rapid steps were approaching on the hard floor. She looked up, the canteen was nearly empty, and Mr Dwyer was hurrying towards them. Not now, she thought.

'Sorry I've been so long. Come along Yola, we'll have our little chat now.'

✦ ✧ ✦

'You see Mr Dwyer, *I* was that mine,' Yola explained. 'My stump was the detonator; the white stuff you were putting on me was the explosive. When Mr Hans, the deminer, pressed

88

down on the trigger I heard it click. I knew he had made the mine safe, but no one had made *me* safe. Then there was the smell of cinnamon … ' Her breathing was getting shallow – she could almost smell the cinnamon – the room was stuffy. Mr Dwyer put up his hand to slow her down.

'There is no hurry, Yola. We have lots of people who have these terrible flashbacks,' he said comfortingly. 'It's nothing to be ashamed of. It's called post-traumatic stress, but we leave that to the experts. What I want to be sure of is that we don't upset you when we make your cast next time.'

Yola wanted to ask if Fintan would be there, that would help, but she didn't like to ask. She said bravely, 'I'm all right now. I'll close my eyes and think of my lovely new leg.'

Mr Dwyer laughed. 'Well, Fintan's achieved something with his morning then. When we get the all-clear from your counsellor we'll have another try.'

11

Airbags for Africa

Abonda, that's her name. Mr Dwyer got me to show her around the labs this morning. It was all a bit stiff at first; I was still feeling bad about her. Then me and Sean did our Riverdance act. We were fine then. Perhaps it's because she's so different, but I found myself telling her things about me that I wouldn't tell to anyone else. I wish I knew her age. Sometimes she is so mature, then suddenly she laughs and it seems like she's about ten.

Yola's nostrils were full of the sharp smell of wood smoke, above and all around her was the *tzik tzik* of the crickets in the hedge surrounding the compound. In her dream she could hear Gabbin shouting to the cattle as he led them home. Managu's great bell clanged; he would be leading with Gabbin walking alongside, talking to the cattle, reminding them of their beauty and how proud they should be of their herd. Yola expected Hans to drive down the hill shortly and she strained to hear the sound of the engine. The cattle appeared, a dun mass beneath a forest of horns, floating on the low cloud of dust rising from their hooves. Gabbin appeared too and stood in the compound entrance, his new spear glinting red in the low sun. He was in charge and liked everyone to see that. Suddenly, with a tightening of her waking muscles, Yola realised that the cattle had changed to men, marching in ragged order. What she had thought were horns were the muzzles of guns. Gabbin was still there, his sturdy little legs spread, a Kalashnikov rifle slung across his back. 'Oh Gabbin!' she cried, sitting up straight in bed, blinking at the white, sterile walls of the ward while her pulse raced. 'Oh Gabbin ...' it was almost a whimper.

The pale light of these oh so early Irish mornings penetrated the curtains, but it was too weak as yet to show any colour. At home, daylight came with a rush at six o'clock. Yola could see Catherine's head resting on her pillow in a pale halo of tousled blonde hair. Then she looked across to where Brigid lay. Two, wide, scared eyes met hers. Did Brigid never sleep? Yola sank back. It had been just a dream.

✦ ✧ ✦

Catherine was waiting behind Yola for the basin, wearing a dressing gown of pink blancmange.

'I'm not jealous, oh no, it's just you make me sick! You were with him for *hours* the other day and now you want to see him *again*! What did you find to talk about? You never say much to me!' Yola glanced at Catherine in the mirror. Catherine saw her and tried to pout, but then her face lit up. 'It must be love: romance in the artificial leg room! Oh go on, do tell me. You'd have the loveliest babies. He's quite dark – they'd be coffee-coloured, I think. If he were fair like me you'd have a problem, they might be mottled, or like Dalmatian puppies, white with black spots, or is it black with white spots, I can't remember.'

Yola, who usually wanted to strangle the girl, found herself laughing into her towel. She did want to see Fintan again – she had to hear the rest of his story – but Catherine's silly talk set alarm bells ringing. She remembered how she had let herself get too fond of Hans.

91

'Stop, Catherine! You can have him all to yourself. You see my marriage is already arranged. I am ... how do you call it? ... engaged. The nephew of a great chief has asked my father for me to marry him.' She thought of Gabbin, dear little Gabbin, but it was worth the half-lie just to see Catherine's reaction.

'Oh!' she said, eyes and mouth like three 'O's as she absorbed this information. 'Is that ... is it romantic? Is he handsome? He'd be black, of course.'

'Oh yes, Catherine, he is as black as me and very handsome.'

'But how ... what? Did he kneel at your feet?'

Yola moved back from the basin to let Catherine in and perched on the edge of Brigid's bed.

'I can tell you all about it. There was a big ceremony at my home. My father was sitting in his great chair and everybody was gathered around, then this handsome young warrior came and stood in front of my father. He had a long spear and he told my father, in front of everyone there, that he wanted to take me to be his first wife.'

'*First* wife!' whispered Catherine.

'Yes. That is important for me, it means that I will always be the senior wife in the compound. When he takes other wives ...'

'*More?*'

'Oh yes, but they will be junior to me and I can boss them around and make them do all the hard work.'

For the first time – possibly ever, Yola thought – Catherine was speechless. Absentmindedly she squirted several inches of multicoloured toothpaste on to her brush. Yola didn't want to elaborate, but Catherine had one more question.

'But do you love him?'

Yola was tempted to say no, but then she sensed that Catherine's faith in life and romance hung in the balance. She thought of Gabbin, how he had saved her life, and how he had stood up in front of everybody and asked Father for her to be his first wife.

'Oh yes, Catherine,' she said, 'I love him very much indeed.'

Catherine nodded gravely. In a moment she would think of some other question, but just now Yola needed her help. 'Would you do a message for me, Catherine?'

'I've got occupational therapy in half an hour,' she mumbled through an eruption of pink foam.

'That's all right, this won't take a minute. I'd like you to take a message to Fintan for me?'

Catherine rinsed vigorously, 'Mmm,' then spat. 'No, curses! I've been banned from the labs – pain of death.'

'If you had a message for Mr Dwyer as well, I'm sure you'd be allowed in. Tell Mr Dwyer that my counsellor says he can do my leg anytime. Then you can ask him if you can have a word with Fintan, I'm sure he'll agree. Just ask Fintan if we could meet in the canteen at lunchtime.'

Catherine wagged her finger severely. 'Remember you are engaged. I'll be watching your behaviour from now on.' She dressed with remarkable speed and skipped off.

The ward was suddenly empty and very quiet. Yola was having misgivings. Why did she want to know about Fintan's life? She stood up, but as she did so, a voice came from the bed behind her.

'She'll tell him you know.'

Yola looked down; it was Brigid. She was still in bed, probably trying to catch up on the sleep she couldn't get at night. Yola felt a pang of conscience, she'd hardly said a word to the girl since she'd come; she'd been so preoccupied with her own affairs. She found a chair and sat down beside Brigid's bed, feeling awkward in front of those too-wide-open eyes. Brigid was older than Yola, seventeen perhaps, it was difficult for her to tell.

'Tell him what?' she asked.

'About your warrior.'

'So you heard?' Yola thought for a moment. 'I think … I hope she will.'

'Don't you like him?'

'Fintan? He's nice, but … well, he's European and I'm African. There's so much I don't know. Just because I speak English, people think I understand, but I don't really. I'm guessing or pretending half the time. I don't want to give him the wrong impression.'

'And your chieftain, your warrior? You love him?'

'Oh yes … he's sweet.' Yola laughed. She glanced at the face beside her, then towards the door. She had to tell someone. 'He's ten years old and just so high.' It was worth it just to see Brigid smile.

Catherine would be with her occupational therapist for an hour now.

'Would you like to hear?'

Yola settled down and told Brigid how she had lost her leg, how Gabbin had saved her life, and how he had astonished everyone by proposing marriage in front of the whole clan. The reason he had proposed, of course, was because no one wanted a wife with only one leg. Then Yola told her about the deminers, and how she hoped to go back and work with them. She even told her a little bit about Hans.

'I swore then …' she said, and stopped. Brigid's eyes were closed; she had talked her to sleep. For the first time almost since she had arrived, Yola felt completely satisfied with herself. She stretched, and got up quietly.

Fintan was late, and Yola was having trouble with her Irish stew. She had eaten the meat and the potato and was now faced with a lot of gravy and no way to get it up to her mouth. She took some bread and squeezed it into a ball, then she pressed her thumb into it to make a cup and tried to scoop up the gravy that way. At the crucial moment it disintegrated. She looked up in despair, to find Fintan looking down at her with an amused expression.

'You're supposed to mash up the potato and get the gravy up that way,' he explained as he offered her a spoon from his tray. 'Sorry I'm late.'

He picked up his knife and fork. 'You are ahead of me. Tell me about Africa while I eat. The only country I know anything about is Kasemba, and that's from the encyclopaedia.'

'But that's where I come from. How do ...' Yola began, but Fintan grinned and waved his fork.

'Later,' he said with his mouth full. 'Plastics – tell you later.'

Fintan was a good listener and kept asking questions that drew her out. By the time he had abandoned his soggy cake in custard, she seemed to have given him her life story.

'But how is it that you know about Kasemba?'

'I mentioned the other day that just when I thought the factory had closed forever, a man had come to my father with a proposal for a contract that would save it. Well, the man's name is Birthistle, and he is the agent for a big European car-maker, which is setting up car assembly plants in the developing countries, one in Asia and one in Africa.' Yola nodded. 'But they have a problem. Because of the rough roads they find that the air bags they fit in their cars sometimes blow up unexpectedly when the car hits a pothole.'

'What are air bags?'

'Air bags are things that are fitted into the dashboard of the

95

car and blow up like a cushion if there is a crash. Instead of going through the windscreen, you bounce off the cushion.' Yola thought of the potholes on the road to Simbada. 'Well, apparently they have an answer to this. It is a little plastic box that can be placed in the car. Inside this box is a microchip, like in a computer, which is sensitive to sound and can be programmed to tell the difference between the sound of a real crash and the sound of a car hitting a pothole. It can tell the difference between almost any sounds – between my flute and your flute, for example. Well, the reason they came to Dad is that these microchips are made in Ireland, but they are not handed over to just anyone. Apparently they can be used in guided missiles or atom bombs or something. If, however, they are made into something peaceful, there is no problem. All Dad has to do is get the necessary licence to make this gadget and the motor company will put up the money to reopen the factory. The reason I know about Kasemba is that that's where they are building their new car plant. They are also building a research station in … Murabende … is it?' Yola frowned. 'Sorry, did I get the name wrong?'

'The name is Murabende all right, but it is a different country. It is just over the river from Nopani, the town where I live. We don't like them because they supported the rebels during our civil war, letting them have training camps and things.' Suddenly, Yola felt she was being churlish. 'This must be good news for your father.'

'It should be, Yola, but there is something wrong. I feel it, but I can't see it.'

'Like when you knew I was screaming just to get attention,' she said ruefully.

'I could hear that and see it!' he laughed. 'I really don't know. It is something to do with Dad's agent, this Mr Birthistle – he's just too good to be true. I like him, but I think I'm frightened of him at the same time.'

'You can mind-read Fintan, you really can. Be careful!'

'What do you mean?'

'I mean be careful of your Mr Bithwistle.'

'Birthistle,' he corrected her absentmindedly. 'I wish you ...' He sighed, and then looked at his watch. 'I'm really sorry Yola, but I have to go soon and tidy up. You see, I'm going home tomorrow.'

Yola was dismayed. This was all wrong; he couldn't just walk out of her life like this. There were so many things unanswered. Before she could stop herself she had blurted out, 'But your flute, you haven't told me.' She had to know what had happened to his flute. 'That's what you really want! To be a musician, a player of the flute, isn't it?'

For a second she thought she had gone too far. He had stopped in the act of getting up and was looking at her as if he were seeing her for the first time. When he spoke, it was quietly and matter of factly.

'He broke it ... Dad ... he broke my flute. He didn't mean to, but he did, it was at the worst time. I drove him to distraction practising. He has a temper and ... well, we were both to blame.'

Yola didn't know what to say, her mouth had gone dry, she dropped her head. 'I'm sorry,' she whispered.

Fintan leaned across the table and lifted her chin. 'Don't be sorry. It's just I haven't been able to tell anyone before, but it's a secret between us, ok?' She forced a smile and nodded. 'I'll come and visit you in Africa!' He was laughing at her now.

Yola wanted to mark the occasion; she opened her purse and, by chance, found one of Hans's business cards. She pulled it out and said grandly, 'Our card!' Something flashed in the light, shot across the table and clattered to the floor. It was the saint's medal that the woman on the plane had given her.

Fintan picked it up.

'That's St Christopher,' he commented, turning the medal over. 'He'll look after you – he looks after travellers.'

He took her hand and pressed the medal into her palm, closing her fingers over it. Picking up Hans's card he said, 'Bye so,' and walked out through the nearly empty canteen.

The Silver Chain

For Christ's sake Fintan, grow up and cop on. She's fourteen, two years younger than you, and she's engaged to a six-foot tall, black warrior and you don't care!

The parallel bars seemed to stretch to infinity before her. She was aware of her new leg because of the suction on her stump. She was about to take her first step on her own.

'Now, look Yola, this is no big deal. Your new leg will feel strange, but really, once you get used to it, it will be just like your old one. Think of it as a friend you are getting to know.'

'It feels far too long, Mr Dwyer,' she complained.

'That's because you've been walking on one leg for so long. Your hip has dropped down on the other side. We will have to lengthen this new leg bit by bit until you are even again.'

She could feel the tension in the room. They were waiting for her, apprehensive perhaps; she had a reputation after all. The physiotherapist put her crutches to one side and stood next to her. There was nothing left for her to do but to try. Looking ahead, as she had been told to, so that her body was in a good posture, she lifted her hip and swung her stump forward. Below her eye-level she saw a foot flash into view. For a split second this appeared to her to be her own, her real foot, returned to her and undamaged. For months and months there had been nothing in that space, no leg, no foot, just the ground. She gave an involuntary gasp; the physiotherapist looked up at her quickly. Taking a measured breath she gripped the parallel bars and pulled her weight on to the new leg. She could feel the soft socket around her stump adjusting and redistributing her weight. She was standing! Amazingly, the mechanical knee did not collapse under her. Her good leg, her right one, came forward as if it approved of the new arrangement; she had taken her first step.

There were murmurs of approval. She could hear the voice of the physiotherapist talking, encouraging and instructing her, but it could have been coming from another planet. She wasn't listening. Another step and confidence came flooding into her. For the next step, however, she tried too hard, and her new leg swung forward in a too-willing stride. Instead of riding over it, she lunged into it and drove her stump painfully into the socket, jarring to a halt. She shook her head in determination and muttered something in Kasembi. Then she pulled the over-enthusiastic leg back.

'Small paces, Yola! Take it easy, rise up over the leg, don't drive into it, ripples for the moment, not waves.'

She was prepared to listen to instructions now. Ripples and not waves, ripples … one step, two, another, and another. She had a rhythm going now and the perspective between the bars was shortening. When she got to the end she had half a mind just to walk off across the room, but the physiotherapist's hand restrained her.

'Go easy, easy, Yola.'

But Yola was flying. She gave the surprised woman a hug of delight. Mr Dwyer came up with a screwdriver to make some adjustments, so she hugged him as well.

'Well, that's all we can do for you now. It's over to you and the physiotherapists.'

◆   ◇   ◆

Yola spent hours in the gym. She had never realised that one walked with one's whole body. She would come back to the ward between sessions too exhausted to read. Any book that interested her had too many words she didn't understand. When Catherine was discharged it was as if the sun had gone in. One evening, Yola collapsed into the chair beside Brigid, undid the screw behind her knee and sighed with relief as the vacuum was released. She must remember that the leg might fall off when she stood up next. She told Brigid about her work on the treadmill and the stepping stones. There was a terrible wobble board thing, like a seesaw, which she worked on, back and forth, in front of a huge mirror so that she could check her posture and balance. Then, simply because she was too tired to think of anything else to say, she said, 'Tell me about yourself Brigid. Tell me about your accident?' She closed her eyes, not really expecting a reply. Everyone knew that Brigid couldn't re-member, or didn't dare to think about it.

Perhaps Yola had dozed off for a second, because suddenly she realised that Brigid was speaking. Not about the hospital, or about Catherine or Fintan, but about the car she had been driving in, and it was going faster and faster.

'I told him to slow down but he said he drove better after a jar.'

Yola wondered what a 'jar' was, but it didn't matter. She dared not move; she hardly dared to breathe. Then Brigid stopped. Go on, Yola willed. It was agonising – if the thread were dropped now, surely Brigid would never start again. Yola remembered how, when she was upset, her mother would lis-ten to her, not saying anything but eeeh ... eeeh. With hardly any breath behind her voice she heard herself imitating the sound, 'eeeh', and then again, 'eeeh'. She knew that to Brigid it was a foreign sound, but she was foreign. I am listening, I am not judging, I am here for you, it said. And so she got Brigid to tell it all. It was as well she was tired and half anaesthetised by her own voice, because what Brigid told of that drive, of her crash and of the hours before her rescue were beyond belief.

'Eeeh,' she said yet again, but Brigid's voice had stopped; this time she had talked herself to sleep.

Later that evening a nurse came into the ward to check on the patients. Yola noticed her staring at Brigid, who was lying in bed on her side, as usual. The nurse went up and listened to her breathing and then turned to Yola with a smile. It was then that Yola noticed what had caught the nurse's professional eye: there was a change in the way the girl was lying. She remembered her very first day in the ward. Catherine had called Brigid ... what was it ... The Hump. Well, the hump was gone; the frightened, defensive knot of fear and anxiety had come undone and Brigid was lying stretched out, full-length, relaxed in sleep like any other girl.

✦ ◇ ✦

It was towards the end of her stay in hospital that Yola received a padded envelope in the post. The postmark was smudged. She opened it in the loo, as the ward was now full of people she didn't know. She pulled out a piece of paper. On it were the words: *For St Christopher. Love F.* There didn't seem to be anything else in the envelope. She tipped it up to be sure, and a silver chain spilled like sand into her palm.

Stormy times at home. I'm not going to have it out with Dad again. He wins. I think I thought that, with the music, the leaving cert. would somehow melt away, but it won't. Plastics win (for now). Mr

Birthistle – of the air bag project – was here when I got home and was in on some of my confrontation with Dad. I must say he was great and came to my support. I don't know why I felt uneasy about him. It's just his way of talking, as if life were some sort of board game. I can go along with this, but Dad hasn't a clue. A spade is a spade to Dad. I told him that Birthistle was hinting that there was more to the air bag project than met the eye. But Dad just snapped at me: 'That man's a fool! I have all the certificates of approval here from every competent authority short of the Pope. I'm not looking for trouble; no more are you boy. In your Grandfather's time ...' There we go, 'Fifty sweaty men ...' blah, blah, blah.

The trouble is Dad doesn't know when he's won. I've been thinking about Yola a lot. I can't just let her walk out of my life like this. I went down town and got her a silver chain for St Christopher. I put it in an envelope with a short note and a big chunk of emotion. Perhaps that's that?

The Hangman's Noose

'Hey! Anyone seen Hopalong?' a cheerful voice rang through the room. 'Oh, Yola,' it went on, 'Mother Hen wants to see you.'

Yola heaved herself to her feet and made for the door. She had abandoned her crutches when indoors but her leg still thumped on the floor. The owner of the cheerful voice, Elaine, held the door for her.

'And remember, it's Mother Superior, Yola, not Mother Hen like last time, ok?'

The door swung to behind Yola and the ripple of laughter was shut off. She just loved being teased. It had started after Christmas, when Elaine had invited her to stay at her house for the holidays. She had learned so much: how to use an electric beater, how to decorate a Christmas tree, how to operate the remote control on the video. Elaine had begun to tease her then. When they got back to school after the holiday, Elaine kept it up and soon the other girls began to tease her too; Yola felt that they had accepted her. A lot of it was over her eagerness for lessons. How could they know what it was like for her to have one class after another, each one more interesting than the next. To feel like ... like the sun-sucked soil when the rains come in huge, spattering drops onto the dry earth. You can even hear a faint hiss from the soil as the first drops are pulled down greedily. Then green shoots begin to heave the crust apart and sudden flowers pop their buds in unexpected bursts of colour.

New ideas burst inside Yola's brain like sudden flowers. She wanted it to go on, it had to go on, but now, just like when the rains fail, it had petered out. She knocked on the polished wooden door of the principal's office. A statue of a saint looked down from a niche above the door. Elaine had assured her that it was St Jude – the saint for lost causes. A voice called her in.

My dear Mother,
When Mother Superior told me that my ticket had come for me to go home I was very sad. But now I have nothing to do because all my friends do exams and there is no class. I did some exams, called Mok and passed some, in Geography I did 'C', which is good for me but I still write too slow.

My friend Elaine asks me to stay with her but I think I must come home to my dear Mother. Sister Attracta will take me to Dublin so I can get some presents. What would Gabbin like and I will not forget mother Sindu. There is no plane to land in Nopani, so I must go on to Simbada. Perhaps I see Isabella there.

I see you, Mother. Your loving daughter,
Yola.

Yola didn't want a window seat. She didn't want to look out. She lifted her new knee with both hands so that it straightened out in to the aisle. It gave a slight click. She sighed; it was silly to have got tearful at the airport.

An airhostess was moving down the aisle offering morning

papers. Yola took a copy of the *Irish Times*; it was the only paper left. A headline on the front page read: *'Major Peace Conference for Ireland'*. In smaller print below this was an explanation: *'Ireland has been chosen as the venue for a major conference on arms limitation to be held in Dublin in October of this year. A spokesman for the International Committee stated yesterday that Ireland's neutrality and non-involvement in arms manufacture has been a major factor in bringing this conference to Ireland.'*

She struggled briefly with the article but was soon defeated. Hans would be interested though, so she slipped the paper into the seat pocket in front of her.

'Cabin crew: arm doors and cross-check.'

She closed her eyes and imagined herself walking importantly across the tarmac, the *Irish Times* under her arm. Hans would be waiting for her. She smoothed away her smile with her hand. A new fear gripped her – perhaps Hans had gone back to Norway, perhaps no one would meet her in Simbada. The man beside her lowered his paper for a moment and she had a brief glimpse of green grass and blue sky in the frame of the window.

'Cabin crew: prepare for take-off.'

It seemed such a short time since she had landed in Dublin, but so much had happened. St Christopher nestled in the hollow of her throat; she ran her fingers over the chain. She was comfortable with her artificial leg now and needed only one crutch to give her confidence. She had had a Christmas card from Fintan showing a pig playing a flute. He said he was busy preparing for his Leaving Certificate. The engines roared and she could feel herself being pressed back into the seat as the plane surged forward; she was on her way home. She had bought Gabbin a nice T-shirt with a map of Ireland, showing the four provinces in bright colours.

◆ ◇ ◆

The long night had passed. The change of engine noise woke her. All but a few of the blinds were drawn against the dawn outside, but Africa was out there! Taking advantage of her aisle seat, she fished her toothpaste and brush out of her flight bag and joined a short queue for the toilets. There was a small port-hole window at the end of the side-aisle and she peered down. Far below, forest rolled like a green carpet. A scratch of red-brown earth marked a road cutting through it like a thread. There were fields and compounds at irregular intervals along the road, but they were flying too high for her to be able to see huts or people. There are people down there, she thought, and it seemed strange to think of them getting up just now to start the day while she was up here.

Gradually the view changed. The forest gave way to a wide chequer of fields, a valley perhaps because a dark river snaked through them. Then, suddenly, Yola recognised where she was and banged her head on the plastic rim of the window as she tried to see more clearly. There, almost directly below, was a town, its streets and houses still in shade, waiting for the sun. But yes, there was the bridge, the two bridges: one for the road, one for the railway. It was Nopani – it was home! If only the plane would sweep her down and land there now!

What really gave it away was the inky ribbon of the river that formed the boundary between Kasemba and Murabende to the north. She could see the Hangman's Noose – a meander in the river so extreme that only a thin strip of land prevented the river cutting straight through its narrow neck. It really did look like a noose from up here.

It was a big area that belonged to Kasemba and had once had over a hundred farms, but now it was empty. Five years ago there were elections in Kasemba and a socialist government was elected. They said they would nationalise oil reserves, and the mineral mines in the north of the country. Political agitators got to work on the people in these mining districts and incited them to rebel. In this way the Kasemba Liberation Army, or KLA, was formed. The KLA received guns and training from the Murabende government by promising them oil and minerals in return – they even promised them the land within the Noose in return for their help. The fighting for Yola's home town, Nopani, had been fierce because it commanded the bridges over the river, and it had been during that fighting that the mine she had stepped on had been laid.

Eventually the KLA were defeated by the government forces. The border with Murabende opened again, but the dispute over the Noose lands lingered on – and not all the rebel guns had been handed in. Before they surrendered, the KLA had laid a dense minefield across the neck of the Noose. Because of this, the hundreds of Kasembans who had fled the fighting could no longer get to their land. Hans was itching to get at that minefield because then the farmers and their families could go back home and work the land again. But because it could cause trouble with Murabende, he was not allowed to touch it.

Yola was about to turn away when she noticed something surprising – she had seen smoke! She pressed her forehead against the window. How could there be smoke down there if no one could pass the minefields? But it was quite clear: a little cluster of fires, threads of smoke rising vertically in the still air before dawn. Who was down there? How had they got there?

✦ ✧ ✦

Yola had just arrived from Simbada airport; she stood in dismay among packing cases and chaos in Isabella's house.

'Don't tear your jeans,' Isabella warned, 'some of those packing cases are sharp! Trust a man to go off and leave his wife to do all the hard work!'

Where was Hans? Yola wondered. Left? Gone to Norway? Where?

'But, Isabella,' she exclaimed, 'where are you going?' This was terrible.

'Haven't you heard?' laughed Isabella, running her fingers through her hair. 'Hans has been promoted. We are opening a Regional Office in Nopani.'

'Oh wow!' exclaimed Yola. 'Oh wow, oh wow,' and she had to laugh at herself; she had thought only Catherine could 'wow' like that. 'Tell me, go on!'

'I'll tell you while we work,' said Isabella. 'I hope you are not too tired. You see, you and I are leaving for Nopani tomorrow.'

Yola wasn't tired then, but she was dropping by the time the packing had been completed. It was such a disadvantage not being able to bend her knee to lift things. When the work was done, they moved out on to the veranda with glasses of coke from the fridge. She watched her glass frost in the warm night air while Isabella filled her in on what had been happening.

'Yes, Hans has got his wish. The Nopani mine problem is bigger than we expected and it's difficult running it from here, running up and down for everything. Also his wife objected – too many pretty girls in Nopani.' Isabella grinned. 'So, Head Office has agreed. He has found an old barracks on the north side of town. There are bunkhouses for the deminers, and the old adjutant's house is an office and there is accommodation for the office staff. Hans and I will be looking for a house in town.'

Yola smiled bravely, but a cloud was descending. She lived

on the south side of the town. If they were on the north, they might as well be on the moon.

'Has the work up at the hill finished then?' she asked.

'Where you found your mine? Yes, that's all clear now.'

'Oh ... good,' but Yola couldn't hide the disappointment in her voice.

'Come on, sad face. What's the matter? I thought you'd be pleased.'

'Oh I am. It's just ... it's so far away. The north side ... well, it's like school all over again. I'll never get across town to see you.'

'Tell me Yola, be honest, were you really hoping to work for us?'

'Well, I did hope, just a little. I thought maybe I could paint sticks like Gabbin did. But now you've gone.'

Isabella got up and walked into the house. She came back out holding an envelope.

'I should have given you this before.'

Ridiculously, Yola wondered if it could be from Fintan. Then she noticed that it had no stamp.

'Hans said to give you this, but said to be sure ... well ... sure that you were interested.'

Yola opened the envelope. She was mystified; it seemed to be full of forms. The pages were white, yellow and blue. Isabella was looking at her with a half-smile.

'Go on, they won't bite.'

Yola wasn't used to forms, but gradually three words resolved themselves. The first was *Contract* and the next were *Yola Abonda*. What was this? Now Isabella was laughing openly.

'There's no need to take it as a death sentence, Yola. I'll explain. You remember that Hans said he would try to find some work for you, a holiday job with us if you wanted it?' Yola nodded. 'Well, NPA is a very professional organisation. Everyone who works, even if it's to work just one day in the week, must have a proper contract. That's what that is.'

'Contract!' whispered Yola in awe. 'So you mean I can work with you all summer? That I can stay in your barracks?'

'Yes, you will stay in the staff house.'

'But Isabella, will it be all right for me to stay there? They are all ...'

'White?' prompted Isabella.

'Yes, I suppose so.'

'Do them good!'

'Oh Isabella, I don't want pay, I really don't.'

'Oh yes you do. Hans insists. You see, if he pays you, he says that he can sack you if you don't do what he says, or if you are lazy. Now that he's the boss up there the power is going to his head, I'm afraid. I'll need you to help me bring him down a peg.'

'Oh my God, Isabella. Where do I sign?'

◆ ◇ ◆

The Landcruiser pulled up at the self-same spot where Hans had waited for Yola and her mother that early morning, months ago.

'Are you sure you are all right to walk?' asked Isabella as she helped her down. They were both stiff after the exhausting drive, but it was so wonderful to be back in Nopani! Yola stretched out her arms wide ... wide. Isabella laughed. 'Are you planning to fly?'

Yola closed her arms about the older woman. 'Oh Isabella ... it's home, that's all.'

'The walk won't be too much?'

'Oh no, I can walk for miles and miles,' lied Yola happily.

Then she added, 'I'm so glad you are both up here now.'

She picked up her flight bag and started up the hill for home. She had done some careful re-packing that morning so that she had only her essentials with her. Isabella was taking her suitcase down to the camp and the adjutant's house.

She reached the entrance of the compound and rested for a moment. A contented hush met her as she struggled up the steep slope to the compound. It was hot. A thread of smoke rose from a dormant cooking fire. Hens were fluffed out like powder puffs in their scratched hollows and a yellow dog looked up at her, assessed her astutely, and lowered his head on to his paws. She approached her mother's hut. The door was open to catch any passing breeze. Yola stepped inside; she could hear her mother's breathing. There was a domed basket upturned on the floor; slender cheepings told her that Mother had a clutch of chicks. That was nice.

She sat down on the edge of the bed – their bed.

'Mother,' she said in a low voice, 'it's me, Yola! Mother, I see you.'

She felt a hand groping for hers. It was rough and hard to the touch. 'Yola, my daughter, you have come. I see you. Eeeh.' And Yola remembered Brigid all those miles away; the last time Yola had seen her, she was sitting up in a chair smiling and talking to a nurse.

Yola did her rounds: Senior Mother, Sindu, the aunts. Her new leg was a source of wonder and she had to show them all the things she could do now. Father came to see her when he came in. She told him about NPA and her job, but he knew all about it. She got the impression that there was very little he did not know. Before he left, he took her face between his hands. They were strong but soft, not like Mother's work-worn hands. He seemed pleased with her.

'You have come home quietly child, that is good,' he said.

When the opportunity arose, Yola slipped into her secret place behind the granary. As she had half expected, there were signs of occupation. Her tin-box was still there; there was something in it. When she left it had been empty. She thought to open it, but decided to put it back. This was Gabbin's private place now. She sat down on the log that he had got for her all that time ago and settled down to wait.

He appeared silently. She had heard the cattle go by shortly before. She just looked up and he was there.

'I haven't touched anything,' she said.

He'd grown, or perhaps just changed. He hadn't brought his spear, clearly he too liked to slip in here unseen.

'Come in, sit down.' She patted the log beside her. He came and sat; nothing said, no smile. He smelled pleasantly of cattle. Then he put out his hand and placed it on her new leg, feeling its solidity beneath her jeans. He turned and looked up at her, the old impish smile spreading across his face. She put an arm over his shoulders and gave him a squeeze.

They talked about his cattle, Managu was lame, and about school – he was going to senior school next year. Then Yola told him about her adventures. He wanted to know all about how her leg was made and what it looked like. She said she would show him when she wasn't wearing jeans.

After the long Irish twilight, darkness came with unexpected speed. Gabbin and she slipped out unseen and parted near Yola's hut.

'Where are you sleeping?' she asked on impulse, as Gabbin left.

'Uncle Banda's – he's back,' said Gabbin.

'Was he away?'

Gabbin shrugged and avoided her eyes.

Yola watched him go and wondered why that news made her uneasy.

✦ ✧ ✦

Yola waited for the Landcruiser to collect her at what she now thought of as Hans's corner. It was early on Monday and she didn't expect Hans to come in person, but he did.

'I just had to come to see that new leg of yours. Come on, show me how you can walk.'

She handed him her crutch and did a small walk-about.

'Is it comfortable?'

'Yes, but it gets a bit hot and slippery – that wasn't a problem in Ireland. I keep on thinking it will fall off, or twist around.'

'But it doesn't?'

'Not yet,' she smiled. They climbed into the jeep.

'You've heard we have the dogs up here now?'

'Yes, but I'm not sure what they do.'

'They are amazing! They are able to smell the tiniest tinge of explosive. So if there is a mine or bomb under the ground, they can smell it right away.'

'But don't they set them off?'

'No. They are too light, also they are trained to sink down and point with their noses. No digging or scrabbling allowed. We'll show you.'

'I think I'm frightened of dogs. Do they bite?'

'Not usually. There's only one that bites. You'll recognise him, he's black and white, the only collie we have. All the others are huge German Shepherds, but they are quiet as lambs. If you are bold, we will send you to sleep in the kennels! But if you are good, you will be sharing a room with Judit, my assistant in the office. She's Dutch and lovely, you'll like her. The only trouble is the room is at the top of the house. Will you manage?'

'To be good?'

'Of course, but I mean to climb the stairs?'

'Try me!'

✦ ✧ ✦

Yola was in seventh heaven.

'Learn about it,' Hans had said. 'Learn about the office, about demining and mines awareness. We will teach you First Aid, and about how we train dogs if you like. But I will pay you so little that you will feel you can walk away at any time.' It was a typical Hans arrangement.

On the first Friday, Judit called Yola in to the office. She said she had arranged a lift home for her for the weekend. Yola thanked her and turned to go.

'Oh, and this is yours Yola.' The Dutch girl handed her a small, square envelope. Yola looked at it.

'Count it if you like!' Judit said, one eyebrow raised.

Then Yola realised – money! – she'd actually been paid. She couldn't believe it. She blundered into the door.

'Thank you, Judit! Thank you.'

'Don't thank me, you've earned it.'

Yola stopped on the way up the hill from Hans's corner and looked to left and right. She slipped off the road and took out the envelope. It peeled open and she slipped out a small wad of notes and some coins. She gazed at it, knowing – just knowing – that no little wad of money would ever mean as much to her again. She counted it carefully and then divided it into three equal folds. She didn't bother about the coins; they'd do her for next week.

When she got to her hut she dropped her flight bag. It was important to act now, while she still had the determination. She walked down to Sindu's hut. Sindu, who had been sleeping, came to the door. Making sure that the girl could see that there were three equal folds of notes, Yola gave one of them to her.

115

'My duty to you, Mother,' she murmured, and stepped back. Sindu quickly counted the notes. Then she shrugged her shoulders and said, 'So little.'

Yola turned, biting her lip. Next she went down to Senior Mother, who gave her a particularly hooded look and the merest shadow of a smile, but she took the money. Mother took hers too, but then gave half of it back to Yola as pocket money.

✦ ◇ ✦

On Monday, she was back at work. She soon learned that what Hans really wanted her to do was to give mines awareness classes. As this involved learning as much as she could about every aspect of landmines and demining, she settled down to hard study, making herself useful when she could.

1 4

Gabbin's Game

Long before the first white men came up the Ruri river in search of slaves, Sister Martha's baobab tree had stood high above its banks. In those days young elephants worked up their muscles trying to push it down, now it took at least ten children holding hands, as they did every term, to encircle its huge, old trunk. The children were on holidays now, so it stood alone and solitary in the middle of the school yard. When Yola was asked where she would like to give her trial class, she said she would like to give it here. It seemed less frightening to have it in her old school; perhaps Sister Martha would be there too. The class, however, would be for the local children and their parents, not for her school friends. Bill, her supervisor, would not take part this time, just take notes on how she was doing. If she passed this test she could then be employed as a junior instructor teaching mines awareness in the villages about the region.

Yola was up at dawn. She viewed the compound. She forced her fingers through her hair. She'd been letting it grow longer because she wanted to straighten it and tie it back, European style, like Isabella's. She had to find Gabbin, she wanted him to help her. She saw a thread of smoke rising from Sindu's hut. If any one knew, Sindu would. Leaving her mother to wake in her own time, she walked down and tapped on Sindu's door.

The door opened and the two girls eyed each other. Sindu's eyes flicked down to Yola's hands – no, this wasn't pay-day – what then?

'I'm looking for Gabbin. He's not with the cousins.' Yola said this more abruptly than she had intended. Sindu would spot her nervousness like a snake locating a mouse.

'What do you want Gabbin for?' the older girl asked. 'Checking up on the behaviour of your future husband? Not before time I may add.'

'I'm not checking up on anyone,' snapped Yola. 'I'm giving my first mines awareness class today and I want Gabbin to help!'

'Oh, so we're turning teacher now. Aren't we good enough for you?'

'Come on Sindu, *you* could give a mines awareness class!'

'Even someone as thick as me, you mean?'

Yola bit her lip. How did Sindu always manage to put her in the wrong? She opened her mouth to try to put things right, but Sindu had a fatter morsel to deliver.

'Gabbin,' she said reflectively, 'your little Gabbin ... he's been in bad company, you know.'

Yola wanted to know, but she was damned if she'd have Sindu criticising Gabbin. 'Oh forget it, Sindu.' She turned on her heel. 'I'll try Senior Mother.'

'But I know where he is.' Sindu had her then; she turned back. 'Please Sindu, I really do need to know now!'

'Well don't forget your manners again. He's with Uncle Banda but ...' Sindu's sense of timing was perfect, stopping Yola in mid-turn. 'But ... Uncle ... Banda ... is ... not ... at ... home!'

Despite her wish to strangle Sindu, a little chill ran down

Yola's spine. Uncle Banda was all right. He had fought with the KLA rebels, but so had many. The war was over now. It was the way that Sindu had said it that was sinister.

'Where is Gabbin then?'

Sindu's gaze slipped past Yola and a thin smile crossed her face. 'There he is now!'

Yola turned. The compound was empty. She heard Sindu close the door behind her. What was going on? She scanned the ground between Uncle Banda's hut and the compound entrance. In the distance she heard the discrete beep of a car horn; that was Bill, her instructor, reminding her not to keep them waiting. Then, out of the corner of her eye, she saw a movement. A small figure darted across the space between two huts.

'Gabbin!' she yelled, 'I need you!'

If anyone had been still asleep in the compound, they were awake now. She'd had enough of mystery. She eyed her small cousin as he approached. He was dressed in army trousers several sizes too large for him and a camouflage jacket.

'What are you wearing that stuff for?' she demanded.

The boy shrugged, avoiding her eyes but glancing towards Senior Mother's hut. A second toot on the horn; they would have to go, enquiries could wait.

'I need you, Gabbin. I'm giving my first class today and I want your help. Will you come?' He nodded, but his eyes were shifting uneasily. 'Well, go and change out of that awful camouflage thing. Put on the T-shirt I got you in Ireland and meet me at the car outside.'

Yola walked towards the compound entrance. Then she stopped. She was being watched. She turned. Senior Mother was standing in the door of her hut. The woman raised her head in a slow, beckoning gesture. Yola went over.

'That boy needs an interest, something to occupy his mind.'

It was on the tip of Yola's tongue to ask why – but one did not question Senior Mother.

Yola only had a minute to wait in the car before Gabbin came trotting down the road, looking like her own Gabbin. He clambered in beside her and let her give him a quick kiss.

'Listen, Gabbin, this is the game I have in mind. It all depends on you.'

✦ ✧ ✦

'I'm a landmine … I'm a landmine …' chanted Gabbin advancing on the children.

Yola's throat was dry from talking. She realised that this game was a risk, but all during her training she had been worried that just by talking about mines, showing pictures, telling stories, she might make the children curious. Would her warnings put them on their guard or merely encourage them to play with mines? How could she get across that they were dangerous? Every year the rains washed mines out of the ground. Some looked like toys, little plastic butterflies that had been scattered from the air. Others looked like tins of food. When she took off her leg to show them how terrible it was to be lame, they just wanted to see how the leg worked. She wanted to get across the message that they must never ever play with mines. When Sister Martha had come up to see how she was getting on, she decided that she would try her game. She explained the rules of the game to them all: Gabbin was a landmine and he would tempt them to play with him, but they must not touch him. She signalled to Gabbin that he could start.

'I'm a landmine … I'm a landmine …' chanted Gabbin as the children moved back, parting when he approached them, wary but amused. 'Come on, play with me,' he taunted.

'Oh no!' chanted the smaller ones. 'Landmines are dangerous, we never play with landmines.'

Yola watched Gabbin apprehensively. What if he could not tempt them to touch him? Then the game would fall flat. Go on! she urged silently, don't let me down Gabbin, please. His circling was changing; he was tempting them, but he was acting too, and the children were responding. This was her old Gabbin! She nearly cheered. While he had been taunting the little ones, he had his back to a group of the older girls – all they could see were the jeering faces of the children in front of him; they couldn't see Gabbin's face. Then he turned, and as he did so, he changed. The naughty urchin disappeared and the bigger girls were presented with a poor, tormented little boy who no one would play with. He ran towards the biggest and softest of the girls. Yola watched her melt and reach out.

'Go on, touch him!' roared the kids in delight. They were supposed to shout 'Don't touch!', but they were getting carried away. The girl jumped back in a lather of embarrassment, while Gabbin, grinning from ear to ear, danced off to find his next victim.

This time he settled on a surly lad with a bashed-about face – the victor of many a fight, Yola guessed.

'Melon face,' jeered Gabbin, doing a monkey act under the boy's nose.

'Go to hell!' the boy muttered.

'What's the matter! Over-ripe?'

The boy snarled and turned away, but Gabbin was in front of him, raising his small backside and chanting, 'Kiss, kiss!'

It was too tempting; the boy drew back his foot.

'Kick him. Kiss, kiss!' roared the kids and the boy skulked off with a face like thunder.

Now Gabbin was offering them his T-shirt. 'Touch me and it's yours.'

Still none of the children had touched him. Perhaps the

game was backfiring, becoming a game of dare? Perhaps Yola should call it off. It was at that moment she noticed Gabbin wince. It was only for a second, a flicker of pain that crossed his face and was gone. She was mystified: surely the big boy hadn't touched him? She glanced across at Sister Martha, who was also looking anxiously at Gabbin; she was frowning and had taken a step forward. Yola decided that it was definitely time to call a halt. She'd wait till Gabbin had passed Sister Martha on his circuit, then she'd ... But then it happened! Gabbin faltered and his hands rose, gripping at that sudden pain in his tummy. His knees gave way and he collapsed onto the ground. A horrified hush fell over the gathering. Yola lurched towards him, but it was Sister Martha who got there first, dropping to his side and lifting his crumpled shoulder.

'BANG!' Gabbin shouted and leapt to his feet.

Yola would remember that frozen scene forever. It should have been, perhaps it was, perfect, better than her wildest dreams. Sister Martha had known the rules, but like Yola – like all of them – she'd been fooled. Gabbin had done exactly what he had been asked to do. The party atmosphere disappeared in a shocked tremor. The class was over. The stunned youngsters trickled away.

But there were other images of that day that Yola would not forget. One was of little Sister Martha reeling back, her hand over her heart, her kind, concerned face drained white with shock. The second was a fleeting look of nasty triumph on Gabbin's face as he leapt to his feet.

The following day, Gabbin disappeared. They said he was visiting Uncle Banda's relations in the next province. Weeks passed, then a month, but no news came back from him. Yola was told not to repeat that game in future classes.

15

The Satellite Phone

'You are in charge then!' said Hans with a grin as he backed into the conference room from the office where Yola was standing. He was balancing a cup and saucer on a stack of files and papers. 'Emergencies only, all right?' The door, which was on a spring, closed behind him with a click and the voices in the next room dimmed abruptly.

Yola looked nervously around the office. Then, being careful not to touch anything, she walked around behind Hans's desk. There was a blotter in the middle of the desk and a stainless steel parrot on a perch. The parrot fixed her with a beady eye. She lowered herself carefully into Hans's chair. It was wonderfully comfortable. Then she found that it swivelled, so she held on to the edge of the desk and swung the chair back and forth. She let go and did a cautious circle. But there was something else that Hans did that looked particularly good; he had some way of leaning backwards. She pressed against the arms, but nothing happened. She pushed against the desk, but the chair just rolled back. Then she leant forwards and swung her weight back into the chair. To her horror, it toppled over backwards. She grabbed at the vanishing desk, missed it and her artificial leg shot up and hit the underside of it with a resounding thump. Waving her arms frantically she threw herself forward but, unfortunately, so did the spring in the chair. As she flew towards the desk she had to look for somewhere to land and skidded to a halt on Hans's blotter.

At that moment she heard a voice at the door. With a speed she hadn't shown since she had two legs of her own, she sprinted out from behind the desk and was looking earnestly out of the window when the door opened. Hans came in, still talking as the door slowly closed behind him, and picked up a file from his desk. Then, out of the corner of her eye, Yola saw him pause. She looked over; her carefully prepared smile froze on her face. Hans's chair was slowly rotating on its beautifully oiled stem while, on the desk, the stainless steel parrot bobbed and twisted, silently squawking out the most serious allegations against her. She could feel her shoulders droop. Hans glanced at her, an amused smile spreading across his face. She shrugged and smiled back weakly. Then the door closed with a click and she was on her own once more.

There was a second desk in the room where Judit, the Dutch girl, usually sat, but she was inside at the conference today. Judit's desk had a subduable chair; Yola sat down, shaking. Then she turned and put her tongue out at the parrot.

She listened to the voice of the radio operator from the radio room down the corridor. It was a stylised call-and-answer routine. He would be talking to any cars that were out and to the deminers who were clearing mines from about Nopani's two border bridges. When Yola had looked down on these from the plane they looked so neat and tidy, but that wasn't how it was on the ground. The men there were working on hands and knees in the dense bush that had grown up since the mines had been laid. Before they could cut even a twig they had to grope ahead with sensitive hands, making sure there were no tripwires attached to mines hidden in the bush beside them.

She shivered slightly and pulled forward a pad of yellow stickers and started writing. When she had finished, she stuck the labels on the two phones in the room. She had been told what to say, but was afraid of forgetting the routine in the heat of the moment. The local phone was all right, she felt she could answer that. It was the satellite phone that frightened her; it might speak to her in Norwegian.

With nothing else to do, she stared out over the old barracks. The huts were empty now that the men were working. At the far end, as far away from the house as possible, were the kennels. She'd got used to the barking now. There were five dogs: four huge German Shepherds, and a black-and-white border collie called Sailor. He was in disgrace as he had bitten two of his Kasemban handlers and now none of them would go near him. Yola would go out and walk him later. She grinned; she and Sailor had a special relationship.

When she had started work with the deminers, Bill, who was English, had shown her around.

'Hans wants you to see everything, so you might as well be fed to the dogs while you are still fat and well-fed.'

Yola's heart sank; she knew he was teasing, but she was nervous of dogs and she didn't always understand Bill's banter. They walked towards the kennels and the dogs set up a cacophony of barking. They were all tied up outside while their kennels were being cleaned. The German Shepherds threw themselves on their ropes as if Yola were the most delicious morsel they had seen in months.

'Don't worry, they just want to play. But watch Sailor there, just because he's quiet doesn't mean that he's safe,' Bill warned. 'We'll have to send him home, he's bitten two handlers already and now no one will work with him.'

'Is he good?'

'At his job? Yes, the best. He's the only one we can trust to pick up tripwires for a start, but the bush is so thick by the river we can't use him there.'

Yola looked at the dog. He was black with a snow-white sailor's collar, and he had pleading eyes that followed Yola as she passed. They went to the far end of the line and Bill calmed the dogs and introduced Yola to each in turn.

It was Yola's fault: Bruce, the biggest German Shepherd, was tied up next to Sailor. He was just being friendly, but that meant putting his paws on Yola's shoulders and licking her face. Yola misinterpreted his lunge and stepped back, right into Sailor's space. For a long time she didn't know quite what had happened. She felt a bang on her leg and heard a yelp. She twisted around and there was the fearsome Sailor, crawling across the ground whining and wagging. Without thinking, Yola bent down and put out her hand. Sailor's first reaction was to cringe, then he began to crawl forward, wagging and whining as if he'd been hit. Yola edged back to where he could no longer lunge at her, but let him lick the back of her hand.

'Be careful!' Bill called. Then he sounded puzzled. 'What's got into him? Did you hit him? It's never had that effect before.'

Yola shook her head; she was concentrating. She stroked his head and ran her hand down onto his neck, ready to snatch it away. He trembled slightly and then rolled over on his back.

'Well, I'll be damned!' said Bill.

That evening when Yola was chatting to Judit and feeling for the valve that would release her leg, her hand slipped down the smooth calf. Suddenly she stopped because she had felt something strange; there were marks in the plastic! Judit came over when she heard Yola's gasp of surprise and they examined the marks together. There, in her leg, was a neat set of tooth-

126

marks. Sailor had at last found a Kasemban that didn't taste nice! They laughed together and agreed that they would say nothing. It was about time the men were brought down a peg or two – let Yola's mastery over Sailor remain a mystery.

From that day, Yola exercised the collie every day. There were grumbles from the men when she joined their training but, as Bill pointed out, a trained dog is worth thousands of pounds. Even though Yola would never be allowed into a live minefield, at least Sailor would not lose his tracking skills.

Yola was startled from her reverie by the telephone ringing. She darted towards Hans's desk where the local phone stood. Panic ... wrong phone! It was the satellite phone ringing. She reached out, then hesitated. Should she call Hans? No, he had said emergencies only. She stared at her yellow sticker, swallowed, lifted the receiver and said in her clearest voice, 'Northern People's Aid, Nopani office. Yola Abonda speaking, can I help you?' She could hear a voice, but in her state of panic she couldn't even decide what language it was speaking. 'Excuse me. Can you say me again?' That didn't sound right, but it gave her a chance to listen properly. Suddenly she jumped in the air. 'Fintan!' she shouted. 'How ... where ... how's Ireland?' She switched the phone to her left ear, hoping she would hear better. 'You're what? ... Where? ... Kasemba! ... You can't be!' She put a hand on the wall to steady herself. She realised then that she was shouting and dropped her voice. 'Go on, tell me.' She couldn't believe what she was hearing; it was so nice to hear his voice. He was explaining that it was to do with his father's business. 'Oh, and I thought you were coming to see me!' she laughed.

'I'm using Dad's mobile,' Fintan's voice sounded tense. 'We ... rather I've been turned back at the bridge on the border. You see, I don't have a visa, we never thought ...'

Yola's mind was racing. What border? Why ring her? Then it dawned on her.

'Fintan,' she interrupted, 'you mean you're in Nopani?'

'Of course I'm in Nopani.'

'But if you're at the border that means you have our nice friendly soldiers pointing their guns at you. What on earth are you doing there?'

'Oh Yola, it's all complicated. Do you remember what I told you about Dad's air bag project?'

'Yes, I remember.'

'Well, we visited the new car assembly plant here, in Kasemba, it's at Port George, on the coast. They showed us around, gave us an expensive lunch and then explained that the people Dad really should be talking to are the boffins in their research laboratory in Murabende.'

'This isn't Murabende, Fintan. Murabende's different country. They eat people over there!'

'I know, the lab is over the border there, but I don't have a visa.' He seemed irritated.

'So what's your Dad going to do?'

'He's had to go on with Mr Birthistle, the chap who set up the contract. There seems to be something terribly urgent about getting our samples to the research laboratory. So I'm on the bridge. They called a taxi, but it hasn't come.'

'Who's with you. How many are you?'

'I'm on my own, Yola.'

'On the bridge! On your own?'

'Yes. I can't walk as I have a stack of Dad's equipment – they wouldn't allow him across with it.'

'Jesus, Mary and Joseph!' said Yola, then laughed out loud at herself. 'Fintan! Stay where you are. Do you hear me? Don't move. There is a big tree with a bench under it. It's in sight of the soldiers at the border, so you'll be safe there. I'll see if I can get down myself, but if not I'll ask someone to pick you up, they are working nearby. Oh, and Fintan, don't leave the tarmac, it's dangerous to step off the road anywhere there. 'Bye.'

She turned around. Hans had come into the room and dropped his files onto the desk with a thump. He yawned; then he leant down and addressed the parrot.

'You can tell me what she's been up to later.'

The wretched bird bobbed up and down knowingly; Yola had to come clean.

◆　◇　◆

Hans had to go to the bridge anyway. The river bank had been heavily mined by both the rebels and the government troops in an attempt to keep control of the border crossing. The Landcruiser pitched off the road and down into the deminers' day camp under the trees. A strip of a hundred metres of bush remained to be cleared between here and the bridge, but a safe path wound through to the bridge end.

'Do you want me to come too?' asked Hans. 'I don't really like taking the car up to the border. Whatever about boys without visas, military-looking vehicles are a no-no near that bridge.'

'I'll be fine,' Yola said. 'The path is clear now, isn't it?'

'Just keep inside the stakes.'

The path had been made safe, and a strip of ground each side of it had been cleared. This was marked with white- and red-topped stakes. Shorter, blue-tipped stakes showed where the deminers had actually lifted mines from within the strip. Yola walked as quickly as she could and tried not to think of these. She had to zigzag to climb the last steep slope up on to the road. She turned towards the bridge and halted.

The dead heat of the day had gone but there was still an hour of daylight left; the evening breeze, sucked in by the over-heated land, fanned reluctantly up the river. Ahead, the bridge hung between its heavy iron girders. A shabby, sandbagged border-post, connected to the world by sagging telephone lines, menaced its nearer end. The thin, painted pole across the road looked fragile, but that was deceptive: the guns up there were real.

The tree where she had told Fintan to wait was huge and scarred by war, but its branches were now a blaze of scarlet blossom. It was a colonial tree, planted to welcome white men in pith helmets. She could see Fintan, leaning forward, his elbows on his knees while his fingers moved on his tiny flute. She watched him, smiling, but wary of herself. He was surrounded by an impressive array of equipment. He didn't look up till she was almost beside him; a look of profound relief crossed his face as he scrambled to his feet. They faced each other like two people tied to stakes, wanting to approach but not being able. Yola broke free first and gave him a quick, rather bony hug.

'Welcome to Nopani,' she said. Then she saw a line of empty Coke cans on the bench. 'Did you drink all those?' she asked in amazement.

'Dad and Birthistle left them for me. I've been here for hours!'

'Come on,' she said, 'we have to carry your stuff to the jeep.'

16

The Arms Game

'Just keep to the path,' Yola called back as she side-stepped down the steep slope from the road. She was carrying Fintan's camera, as it was light. 'This is the best part of the day. The heat has gone, work is over and I'm starving!'

She was in a hurry in case Hans was waiting for them, so she let Fintan follow slowly with the rest of his stuff. She was looking forward to showing him around. Hans had said Fintan could have the spare bed in the sickbay if he needed one.

The jeep came into view and she squinted against the reflection on the window to see if there were any sign of Hans, but he hadn't come back yet; they could relax. She turned around. The path was empty. Surely Fintan had followed her? Then, with a stab of apprehension, she saw a pile of bags and cases in the middle of the path. Fintan was not in sight. She couldn't believe it! He must have walked off the demined strip into the bushes.

'Fintan, *stop*!' she screamed, running frantically back down the path, her lopsided gait not helped by the swinging camera. 'Don't move, not a step, not an inch! *Stop*!' She could see him. He was beside a tree, turning towards her, a look of astonishment on his face.

'What's the matter?' he asked.

'The matter, Fintan O'Farrell, is that you are in the middle of a live minefield!'

'But they can't be everywhere, Yola?'

'Yes, they are! That's what a minefield is. I should have shown you. The red and white stakes show where the mines start. Look, you see those blue stakes,' Yola's voice cracked, 'that's where we've actually taken up mines.' She wanted to close her eyes against what she was seeing, then Fintan stirred. '*Don't* move your feet!' she gasped. 'You see that line of stakes? They often lay mines in lines. There: one ... two ... three ... and look where the next one will be.'

Fintan put his hand out to steady himself against the tree. She could see him calculating the distances. If the soldiers had kept to a straight line and spacing, Fintan had just stepped on the fourth mine in the line.

'Why did you go in there?' she wailed.

'I wanted ...' Fintan winced, '... I wanted a pee!'

Perhaps it was the relief that he was safe and that he hadn't stepped on a mine, but Yola's laugh rang out loud and clear. Fintan, however, was in trouble.

'Yola, excuse me, I still need to go ... like, urgently!'

Yola wiped her eyes with the back of her hand and asked innocently, 'Should I go then?'

'Oh yes, Yola, please!'

Frightened that he really might move, she relented.

'All right, but be considerate where you aim. Then we'll have to get you back safely onto the path. I'll see if there's a mine detector in the car.'

There were two, in fact. She took one out and held the sensitive disk over the car keys to test it, but got no response. She tried the other – no response either. If neither were working, she was badly stuck. They might have to go all the way back to

132

the barracks to get more equipment – while Fintan stood motionless and terrified among live mines. Then she remembered that the deminers had to tune the detectors first. She searched for the tuning knob, found it and sighed with relief when the familiar shriek rang out.

Fintan hadn't moved and was looking more comfortable when she got back. He was standing about three paces from the path. She measured a meter-wide strip and commenced sweeping over the ground with the mine detector; it was a little like using a vacuum cleaner, but holding a disk about an inch above the ground. Fortunately, Fintan had chosen a place where the grass was short, starved of light and nutrients by the tree. Yola edged forward. She was now in the minefield – if she got something wrong they could both be blown sky high. At the first shriek they both froze. She brushed gently at the ground with her hand. She could see the corner of a cartridge case. She marked the place; she wasn't going to risk touching it. Then she began her slow advance again. A telephone started ringing, how could there be a telephone here? She shook her head, the ringing was coming from behind her. She felt totally disorientated. Fintan woke up to the sound.

'Yola, that's Dad's mobile phone. It's in my bag there. It may be him. He'll be worried.' It kept ringing while Yola retreated.

'Throw it,' Fintan called.

Yola got as close to him as she could and threw. Fintan caught it and pressed a button. She heard a man's voice. Fintan smiled.

'Hello, Dad. Yes, yes, I'm fine. The taxi didn't come. I'm with my friend … Yes, it did feel a bit dodgy on the bridge, didn't it, but I'm quite safe now.'

Yola had to put her hand over her mouth. The voice on the phone came to her like a dog barking.

'The day after tomorrow ... in the Palace Hotel ... I'll be there. Bye.'

They looked at each other. Yola was ready to splutter with laughter, but Fintan was serious.

'Well, at least he hasn't me to worry about!' he said.

Yola was only a short pace from Fintan when the mine detector shrieked again. It could be anything she told herself, a steel button even. She brushed gently at the loose soil and twigs on the surface. If she had uncovered a snake she couldn't have pulled her hand back faster. There it was, two-thirds covered with soil, probably pushed up to the surface by a root, a little shoulder of green plastic, a mine. She felt sick, waves of fear and relief broke over her. She looked up at Fintan and smiled bravely; the cinnamon scent was thick in her nostrils – she mustn't faint. Fintan's foot must have fallen within inches of the mine.

✦　◇　✦

Yola and Fintan sat out together in the velvet night and watched the stars. They had had a meal in a café on the way back from the bridge, and Hans had talked to Fintan about their work. Yola had enjoyed hearing their voices together, enthusiastic at first. She loved eating out, as she couldn't normally afford it, so she concentrated on her meal and hoped that Hans would pay. It was only when she heard Hans say, 'You must be tired,' that she realised Fintan had gone silent. It was a small incident, but now, as she leaned back to bathe her eyes in the great sweep of the Milky Way, she remembered it.

'Fintan,' she asked. 'What's bothering you?'

His answer was so slow coming that Yola wondered how many stars she could count before he replied.

'I think Dad's in trouble.' She half turned. Then Fintan went on dismissively, 'but I've no real evidence.'

'Go on,' she said.

Fintan sighed. 'Dad and me and Mr Birthistle – you remember who Mr Birthistle is?' Yola said she did. 'Well, we were together in a row of three on the plane, we'd asked for that, but the plane wasn't full. I was really tired but I couldn't get comfortable. My head kept falling forward with a jerk and waking me up. Then I noticed an empty row of three seats on the far side of the cabin. Dad and Mr Birthistle were asleep, so I took my blanket and slipped into the empty seats. There was a partition in front and just one man in the row behind. When I pushed up the armrests I could lie down full length.

'I thought all I had to do was close my eyes and wake up in Africa. After a while, I felt the seat shake; someone had joined the man behind. Then, just as I was on the edge of sleep again, I became aware of their voices. I was intrigued, it sounded as if they were playing a game.' Fintan paused while he thought. 'There is a board game called Monopoly–?'

'Catherine taught me,' Yola interrupted, 'I bought Shrewsbury Avenue and ended up in prison!'

'Yes, that's the official version. But their game was different; it was worldwide – countries, not streets. I thought they might be devising a game for kids. Then one of them said, "Yes, that's how I got my break. Selling toys to the owner of a banana plantation, a real Treasure Chest card. This guy had labour problems so I sold him a lucky bag, just a few worn out ex-Soviet rifles, but it solved his labour problems." What's this about rifles? I wondered. Then he went on, "These people are cute; the rifles worked so well he decided he also had neighbour problems. I got him some real wind-up toys for that, AK47s mostly, but at three hundred rounds a minute they certainly solved his problems with the neighbours. He'll be the next president of his country. But children forget Santa soon enough, don't they? Doesn't want to know me now."

'Yola, it was all so plausible, as if they really were selling toys! They couldn't be serious. Just as I was drifting off, one of them said: "OK, my throw …" and I remember thinking that there was something familiar about that voice. Then, in my dreams, I became a player in their fantasy board game. I raised an army and started buying weapons for it.' Fintan stirred uneasily. 'I can't have slept for long because I suddenly realised I was listening to that familiar voice again.'

'"OK my friend, you tell me you have just drawn a Treasure Chest card and you've a thousand out of date rifles. You could sell these for scrap, collect £1,000. But just think: aren't there kids on the block who would like these? Why not be charitable, why not donate them to a good cause? Cast your bread on the water, as the Bible says. What about the Kasemban Liberation Army?'

Yola jerked upright, 'Hey, the KLA is finished!'

'Not if Mr Birthistle has anything to do with it.'

'Mr Birthistle?'

'Yes. It was then that I recognised the voice. It was none other than our Mr Birthistle. Yola, he's an arms dealer!'

'Are you sure?' she asked.

Fintan looked at her grimly. 'Yes, I am sure, and your saying that the KLA actually exists clinches it. I lay there, not daring to look, just listening. Birthistle went on: "Just think what you can do by being generous. If you give the KLA the weapons they need for their noble cause, we can start a small war."'

'It's not a noble cause!' Yola muttered.

'Listen to what he said: "Soon they will need more weapons, ammunition perhaps, and then more expensive toys; only this time they will pay. But you must be fair – the Kasemban government will also need our guns, so they can fight the KLA.

They've got money for their schools programme that they can spend on weapons, and we can easily get these from the European manufacturers. The Europeans need the income to pay for their Star Wars weapons. You see, civilised people don't want to fight anymore. It's nicer to watch wars on television."'

'Why didn't you stand up and announce him?' demanded Yola.

'Denounce him, you mean ... To a pitch dark plane somewhere over the Sahara? I was horrified, but I wanted to sleep; there was nothing I could do. I woke when I smelled breakfast. When I got up, I looked at once but there was no one in the seat behind mine, and when I got back to Dad, there was Mr Birthistle asleep, apparently, as I had left him. The whole thing seemed too improbable for words. I had a headache and decided then that the whole thing must have been a dream.'

Yola looked secretly at Fintan in the glimmer from the stars, his face was etched and tired, she did like him, but she was worried by his talk about dreaming. Her people believed that their ancestors could speak to them in dreams. Then he went on.

'After breakfast, Birthistle wanted to show Dad some papers, but he had lost his glasses. "Blind without them, boy!" There was a lot of hunting around, then he seemed to remember where they were and made off across the aisles. I stood up to see where he was going. Yola, he went straight to the seat behind the one where I'd been sleeping! It was a shock, but there were no doubts in my mind now. I had liked Birthistle. He had adopted me as a sort of son; he wants me to marry his daughter, Becky. But it all fits – he never answers a question directly, he always replies with a little story. The Arms Game is his way of fooling people into thinking he's harmless, but he's not. He's evil, and he's here on evil business.'

'You mean with your Dad?'

'Christ, no. Dad's a complete pacifist, and the airbag project is life-saving, everyone says so. No. What Birthistle is doing is using Dad as a cover to get a visa into Murabende; he has some other purpose, and now I can't watch him. I didn't expect to be thrown out at the border and I haven't warned Dad.'

'Hans knows a lot about the arms trade, you should talk to him. All I can tell you about is mines, but I can show you around, would you like that?'

'Mmm, yes, I would. Let's stop talking about it now. Isn't it quiet.'

They sat close, but not touching, and the silence of the night wrapped itself around them. An African silence as full of tiny sounds as the black night sky was full of stars. Yola leaned back and told him a story from the dry south of her country, where an ancient people lived who said that on a really silent night you could hear the hunting cries of the stars.

17

Operating Theatre

*I couldn't believe it. I looked up and she was standing there look-
ing down at me. Well, it is a year. I suppose – but she's a young
woman now. I didn't know what to say. It felt good, the two of us just
now outside, sitting together in the dark ...*

'What time is it?' the body in the bed complained.
'It is the first hour in the day, that is six o'clock to
you, and we have to exercise Sailor.'
'Who's Sailor?' The body was stirring now, so Yola retreated.
'Sailor is my dog – well, not really *my* dog – but I exercise
him because no one else will; he eats people.'
'Talking of eating ...'
'Later. We exercise the dogs first while it is still cool. I'll see
you outside.'
Yola sat down on an upturned bucket beside the sickbay,
where Fintan was sleeping, and watched the morning activities
around her. The deminers were emerging from the barrack
huts, polishing their boots and brushing the red mud from
their overalls; they looked smart. Yola breathed in the cool
sharpness of the morning air. The deminers were just preparing for their morning parade when Fintan emerged looking

139

tousled. He looked over to where the men were lining up.

'My God, it looks like an army parade! I'd better comb my hair!'

They walked down the line of huts to the kennels at the far end. The barking rose to a frenzy as they approached. The Kasemban handlers seemed to be fighting and struggling with their dogs.

'Those Alsatians, they're huge!' murmured Fintan apprehensively.

'German Shepherds they call them. They are playing now.'

One of the men shouted to Yola in English as they approached.

'Hey, Miss Yola, I see you've brought Sailor some breakfast.'

'What does he mean?' asked Fintan suspiciously.

'You are the breakfast,' she laughed.

A black-and-white collie had his paws up on the mesh and was barking with the rest when they arrived. When he saw Fintan however, he fell silent.

'Careful,' said Yola, 'I don't trust him when he goes silent like that.'

'But he's just like Prince, the dog on my uncle's farm!' exclaimed Fintan. He put two fingers in his mouth and produced a sharp whistle. To Yola's surprise, Sailor jumped at the wire and barked.

'Look! His tail wagged. How did you do that?' asked Yola.

'Years of practice!'

'Show me how.'

Fintan whistled again, this time a falling note. Sailor sank to the ground.

'Sailor, what sins do you have in your past?' He turned to Yola. 'He was probably a sheep dog that got a taste for sheep.'

'Now he has a taste for Kasembans,' chuckled Yola.

Fintan stepped back sensibly while Yola opened the pen and put the dog on a leash.

'Don't confuse him with whistles now,' she said. 'Let's give him time to get used to you. This is his toy.' She held up the chewed remains of a rubber bear. 'He gets a game when he's a good dog, don't you Sailor … Down, Sailor! Down!'

'How do the dogs work?' Fintan asked.

'I'll show you in a moment.'

They walked in file down a path through thick grass to a place where the grass had been cut back.

'This is where I put Sailor through his paces,' Yola explained. 'I'll put him on his long lead now, and you can watch.' She snapped the lead on to his collar, ruffled his head, stepped back and told him to walk. 'You see, Fintan,' she whispered, 'I must be able to stop him instantly. Let's say I've seen a trip-wire above him.' She called out and Sailor froze in his tracks. Then she issued another command and he sank down and backed cautiously towards her. 'See – he's safe now.'

'Do lots of dogs get hurt?'

'I've never heard of one. Because they are on four paws they are too light to set a mine off on their own. As the handler's in danger too, they are terribly careful.'

'What does he do if he smells a mine?'

'I'll show you with a real one in a moment.' Fintan looked startled. 'It's all right, they are safe now, the detonators have been removed,' she laughed. 'Dogs that look for drugs and things are trained to bark and scrabble when they get a scent, that's their nature – like hunting rats. A demining dog has to go completely against its nature and stay calm.'

There was a place where a large square had been marked off with stakes.

'I'll show you how he searches now. There is a mine planted in here somewhere.'

As Yola concentrated on Sailor, she sensed that Fintan was beginning to relax, fascinated by the search. She kept the dog under strict control. She was using the figure of eight search pattern. Sailor would sweep the ground to her left, nose down, sniffing every inch of the ground, then he would loop around and pass in front of her to sweep a similar loop to her right. They progressed forward steadily. She didn't know where the mine had been laid and was getting anxious when suddenly Sailor circled and sank to the ground.

'Got it!' she whispered. 'What I do now is walk out over the area that Sailor has shown is safe, and mark where he's pointing with this marker.'

She threw the marker. Then she gave a yip and held her arms out. Sailor, who had been whining with excitement, jumped clean into her arms. She produced his rubber bear, threw it for him and then had a deadly tussle for possession. They were both panting when Yola eventually got him to give it up.

'Come on Fintan, there's a tree over there, let's sit under that and talk.'

She told Fintan about her training with the deminers and how her real job was to give mines awareness talks. She was going to tell him about Gabbin and the game he had played on poor Sister Martha, but she could feel her little knot of worry about Gabbin tightening. Anyway, Fintan had worries of his own.

✦ ✧ ✦

Breakfast, and she was aware of Fintan looking with apprehension at the maize porridge she was preparing, but Judit rescued him.

'If you don't like that dreadful stuff of Yola's, Fintan, I have

142

some muesli here. There's dried milk through it so you only have to add water, but make sure the water is from the filter or you'll have the runs for a week.'

Yola sniffed scornfully as Fintan sidled away to take up Judit's offer.

'Oh Judit,' she called, as the other girl left the kitchen, 'Fintan wants to talk to Hans about the arms trade and I'd like to show him Hans's collection of mines and bombs.'

'Not this morning. I've got to make Hans do some serious work today. There's a Dutch delegation coming up to see how we are spending their money.'

'Ok, we'll go down to the bridge and I'll show him what's going on there.' She turned to Fintan. 'I'm on holiday. Hans has given me a few days off. You can bring that camera thing of your Dad's if you want, only don't point it at soldiers on the bridge.'

They walked down through the town together, past the Palace Hotel with its swanky cars outside. As they approached the river, the houses were shell-shattered, some a mere lacework of toppling masonry. In the distance there was an explosion. They both stopped while Yola tried to locate its direction.

'What was it?' Fintan asked. 'A gun?'

Yola shook her head. 'No, more like a mine, I'm afraid, but it wasn't from the river where the men are working. It seemed to come from the fields over there. Often cattle set them off.'

They stepped over the rusted tracks of the railway line, crossed the road and followed the track into the bush to where the deminers were working. They heard excited voices ahead; Yola gripped Fintan's arm.

'Come on! Perhaps I was wrong and something has happened here.'

They hurried forward; a small group was approaching. Yola

recognised the NPA's paramedic, who was leading one of the deminers – still wearing his visor and protective jacket.

'It *was* a snake!' the man protested. 'How could I see in bushes like that. I was feeling ahead, looking for tripwires, gently, gently, when I get bitten.' Sure enough there were two pricks on the back of his hand, now beading blood.

'You should wear your gloves!' the supervisor snapped.

Suddenly the man was screaming. Here he was dying of snakebite and he was being told to wear gloves! The paramedic shrugged. The supervisor scratched his head. Then he saw Yola.

'Yola, go up with this man to the hospital and have him seen to.'

'But I'm on leave!' Yola protested.

'Look Miss, if I or the medic leaves the site, work stops. Be a good girl and take him.'

Yola looked around for Fintan and found herself looking into the eye of a video camera. She made a face.

'Come on Fintan, we'll go with him. The driver will take us. They have a snakebite unit in the hospital, they'll know what to do.'

✦　✧　✦

'I haven't been back to the hospital since my accident. I wonder how it will feel?'

In fact, once they had delivered their patient, Yola found herself full of curiosity to see the place again, and took Fintan on a guided tour.

'It's a bit different to Dublin,' she said apologetically when she noticed that Fintan had a handkerchief to his nose. Yola found the bed she had occupied and where her mother had looked after her so well. She looked up at the slowly rotating fan and noticed with a smile that there was a fly on one of the blades. The bed was now occupied by an old woman, an even older man sat beside her. It was unusual for a man to be looking after someone in the wards. Perhaps there was no one else to feed and tend the woman. She smiled down at the old man, but his eyes were too full of sadness to respond.

'Come on! We can get out this way, past the operating theatre.'

They were halfway down the corridor when the double doors at the far end were thrown back.

'Out of the way! Out of the way!'

A stretcher was pushed through the doors. The porter backed towards them, holding a drip above his head.

'Take her into number one!'

This time the urgent shout came from behind them. Yola turned and collided with Fintan. For a fleeting moment she recognised the face of her own surgeon rushing down the corridor towards them, but they were blocking his way. Swivelling quickly, she noticed a door beside them. A peeling notice said 'Medical students and staff only'. She tried the handle. The door gave way and they both half fell through it as the trolley swept past. For a moment they looked directly into the face of the patient; it was a child, wide-eyed and conscious. Then the door swung shut and they were left alone in semi-darkness. They were in a short passage at the foot of a steep flight of stairs; weak light filtered down from an open door at the top. Yola felt disorientated because she could hear the voice of the surgeon from up above, urgently asking for clamps. Then she realised that there must be some connection between whatever was at the top of the stairs and the operating theatre. Fintan slipped past her, his face set. This was a new Fintan, one she hadn't seen before. He mounted the stairs without making a sound, his video camera in his right hand. She followed, though it was more difficult for her to move quietly with her artificial leg.

They emerged into a gallery, looking down into the operating theatre. There, directly below them, in a vivid pool of light, was the operating table. The child they had seen in the corridor was just being lifted on to it. Yola didn't know what to do. She was pulled by emotions this way and that; she wanted to run, to scream, to stay. She turned. What was Fintan doing? He was staring down, transfixed. As she watched, very slowly, almost as if he had no control over himself, he brought his video camera up to his eye. She saw his finger curl over the handle and a little red light blinked. For a second or two, she rebelled. Was this just another violation of the child below? She, Yola, had been down there, she knew! Then she realised that Fintan was right – someone had to see this, but not her. She sank to the floor with her back to the gallery wall and switched her mind off the scene below. Time passed. Fintan put a new cassette into the camera and filmed on.

Yola emerged from her isolation when she realised that Fintan had turned and, like her, was sitting on the floor.

'Is it over?' she whispered.

'Yes.' His voice sounded hollow.

'Is she alive?'

'I don't know. You see, her own bones have pierced … her own bones … Oh God, Yola … I saw it all.'

Yola thought he was crying. She put her arms around him and pressed her forehead against his chest. When his breathing was even again they went out.

The car had gone back to the river. If the deminer had been bitten by a snake, it was a harmless one they were told. They set out together for the barracks in silence.

I have no appetite for lunch, I ate a banana because she said to, and I've drunk a whole bottle of tepid water from the filter. I can't get the operation out of my mind. It is all real now, too real even to think about, but at the time it was different. I was in some other state of consciousness. It was as if Dad's camera were suspended from the ceiling. My knees wanted to give way, but the camera was holding me up. I wanted to turn it from the scene below, but whenever I tried, it swung me back as if it were the needle of a compass – pulling. I could feel my hands working – focus – zoom – lock the trigger – but these were the camera's commands, not mine. I wasn't there at all; I was having visions of Ireland. There was red – so much red, but I wasn't looking at blood but at a sunset, one of our beautiful lingering sunsets on holiday somewhere in Connemara. Black clouds trailed veils of red over small lakes glistening scarlet, newly wet. Her little white bones became the straight lines of vapour trails in the sky – New York – Boston. I was looking down at my own toes paddling in a peat brown stream, watching them wriggle in the refracting water. But – here was the difference – my toes and my feet were still a part of me. Before they put a mask on her I saw her face, only for a second, looking up at me from the operating table, conscious and alert. And I was back in the canteen at the clinic in Dublin just after I had first met Yola and everyone was staring at us because she had just laughed out loud; then the child's face was obscured by tubes and masks. I think I knew even then that she was going to die.

This is evidence of ... God knows what ... man's inhumanity to man perhaps. I've broken out the tabs on the cassettes. No one is ever going to record over these, but equally I know that I will never be able to look at them again. They did not take her to a ward, but to a shed away from the main buildings. That's how Yola knew that she had died. It looked a lonely place to go, but from what I saw, I think I'm glad.

Bubble Wrap

After a lunch during which neither of them had a will to talk, Fintan went to his bed in the sickbay. When he realised that sleep would not come, he decided to write in his diary. He put his notebook away when Yola came in.

'You should have left the door open. You're supposed to sleep after lunch, not write!' she said as she sat down beside him on the bed.

'I had to, Yola, else that poor child will haunt me forever.' He stared up at the ghostly shroud of the mosquito net hanging above the adjacent bed. 'We have no idea in Ireland, even though we have been blowing each other up for seventy years. We hear of deaths but never think of the process of ... of dying. The injured are hardly even statistics; we forget about them.'

He picked up her hand and held it, looking at it as if he'd never seen a hand before.

'You remember Sam, in the clinic? "Beautiful," he said, "like polished mahogany." And we just blast people to pieces.' He gave her hand back with a small caress and stood up. 'Sorry, I keep forgetting.' Yola was puzzled but Fintan had got up. 'Judit said your Mr Hans would see me now, should we go? Take me to your leader!'

Yola reached up for a hand. He helped her up.

♦ ◇ ♦

The cool of the air-conditioning hit them almost as a chill when they opened the door of the adjutant's house. Yola knocked and Hans jumped up when they came in; he came around to shake Fintan's hand. Yola watched them: the tall, fair Norwegian and the shorter, darker Irish boy.

'Well, Yola, are you going to explain these things to Fintan?' Then, to Fintan, 'She can, you know. One of our budding mines awareness instructors.'

'No way, Hans! You forget I am on holiday. You can't order me around today.'

She smiled at him, and went over to the window. It was peaceful outside. The dogs were sleeping out the heat of the day. The men at the bridge would be working through though – hour on, hour off. In the compound back at home it would be rest time too. She thought Gabbin might be in her secret place. Then she remembered that Gabbin had gone away. Why couldn't these worries leave her alone? They said at home that he was with Uncle Banda, visiting relatives, but he had been away for a whole month! Sindu knew something, but she wasn't saying. She forgot about Gabbin easily enough when he was around, but as soon as he was away there was a small Gabbin-shaped hole in her life.

'We'll start over here,' Hans was saying. 'These are the UXOs, the unexploded ordnance, things like mortars and rockets that never went off.'

Yola knew the routine, first these, then the big anti-tank mines looking like covered dinners on a plate, then the bounding mines that hopped up out of the ground to explode at waist-level, the little anti-personnel mines, like the one she had stood on, were on the last shelf. She listened for a moment, then turned her gaze to the window again. She could see the watchman sitting in the shade, leaning against the wall below. She opened the window and the sound of his radio came up to her.

'What's new, Abdul?' she called.

He looked up with a start. 'Eeeh, Miss Yola, I thought you were the voice of Allah. There is more trouble with Murabende,' he went on. 'Our government's soldiers are going to clear the mines from the Noose, but the Murabendans say that this is their land and it must stay empty until the dispute is settled. There will be trouble.'

Yola remembered how she had looked down from the air on that loop of river and the tract of land it enclosed. There had been people there then: were they local Kasemban people who had crept in, or invading Murabendans?

'You're too gloomy Abdul, and since when did Allah speak with the voice of a girl?' She heard the old man chuckle as she closed the window.

'Look, I'll open it,' she heard Hans say. 'So, here goes the trigger in this little tube. The detonator clips in here.'

Yola smiled, remembering the first day Hans had shown her a landmine. Suddenly she realised that Hans had stopped talking. The room was full of an unnatural silence. She turned. Hans was staring at Fintan, who was holding the open halves of one of the little anti-personnel mines. His face had gone white, his mouth was moving, but no words were coming out. He swayed. Hans moved quickly, held him and lowered him into a chair.

'Put your head between your knees, Fintan! Yola, water – quick!'

✦   ✧   ✦

They sat around the table in the conference room: Hans, Yola, Judit, who had walked in from her siesta in the middle of the crisis, and Fintan. Hans and Fintan were wet.

'You said "Throw it", so I did,' said Yola ruefully.

In the end, Fintan didn't actually faint. But Hans sent Yola with him when he insisted on getting something from his baggage. He rummaged in a holdall, pulling out a spaghetti of coloured wires and bits of electrical equipment.

'I can't believe it ... I can't believe it. Dad – of all people. It's here somewhere. Our first prototype.' Then he reached deep into a corner. 'Got it!' He straightened up, holding a bubble-wrapped ball in his hand. 'Come on Yola, this is when you decide that you never knew me.'

Hans slit the tape. The four of them leaned forward as the wrapping fell apart. It looked perfectly innocent: a small plastic box with a domed top. There was an embossed picture of a stylised car on the lid.

'Oh, so this is the air bag stabiliser you've been telling me about,' said Hans.

'Yes, sir. This is O'Farrell Engineering's new air bag stabiliser.' Fintan's voice was harsh with irony. 'If I may borrow your penknife, I'll show you.'

He inserted the tip of his kife, gave a twist and the box opened. Yola heard Hans draw his breath in sharply, but she still couldn't understand what was going on. The box was empty, just a plastic box with little compartments and something that looked like a black beetle.

'But–' she said.

'Look Yola, look now!' Fintan was holding the little anti-personnel mine beside the air bag stabiliser. 'I'm seeing this for the first time too, remember.'

Suddenly she realised what the fuss was about. The insides were the same – the place for the trigger, the detonator ... all there. It was a landmine. It was her turn to want to sit down.

Fintan turned to Hans. 'But what is the microchip for? It is programmed to tell the difference between a pothole and a crash.'

'You say it is programmed for a crash, but is it? These chips can be programmed for anything. What's this?' Hans picked up a tape cassette that was also in the bubble wrap. 'The answer is probably here.'

He fished in his desk, pulled out a walkman and dropped the tape into it. A few seconds' silence, then the clicks, buzzes and screeches began.

'Recognise that, Yola? That's the sound our present detectors make.' Then the sound changed. 'That's the one the army uses! Hear? Much more click to it. My God, they are all here!' He clicked off the tape recorder and shook his head slowly. 'We've been dreading this, Fintan. This chip has been programmed to listen for the sound of just about every mine detector except, perhaps, the one they use themselves. This is designed specifically to get us. Don't you see, if there is just one of these in an area, or even if we think there might be one, we can no longer work. Mine detectors are out! I don't know what your part in this is, Fintan, but I need coffee, then we will talk.'

19

An Inhumane Weapon

Hans drummed his fingers on the table. Fintan was helping himself to water from the filter. He had been talking for some time, telling them about the whole air bag project and answering their questions.

'They said that the tape was just for test purposes. That's why it had all those strange sounds on it.'

'Ya, so. First,' Hans said, 'this is a landmine, there is absolutely no doubt about that. All the architecture is here: a place for the trigger, slots for the detonator and the explosive. Fintan, you must understand this. What you have here is an inhumane weapon that is banned by international agreement. There are nearly one hundred million landmines in the world, buried in the ground, waiting for people like Yola to step on them – these must be cleared using mine detectors. This mine is designed to kill deminers by exploding when their mine detectors pass over it. Because it is designed to prevent mine clearance, it is doubly inhumane. I must ask you this one question: does your father know what he is producing?'

There wasn't a sound in the room. Fintan picked up his glass of water, but his hands were shaking. He put the water down and pressed them onto the polished surface. When he replied, he did so carefully and precisely, measuring his words.

'No, I don't think he does. As I told Yola last night, I have always thought of Dad as scrupulously honest. He got the design from the car company or whatever they are – picture of the car on top and all. Look, it even shows where the stabiliser is to be fitted! Then he got permission from the Irish government and from then on didn't want to know anything more. His one objective is to get his men back to work.'

'If he is not behind this, who is?'

'That's what I wanted to talk to you about before … before I realised …'

'Tell him about your dream,' said Yola.

This time, Fintan told the story as straight as he could.

✦ ✧ ✦

Hans got up and walked to the window.

'When are Birthistle and your father due back?'

'Tonight.'

'Do they know you have been with us, with a demining organisation?'

'No, I just said I was with a friend.'

'Go Fintan, explain it all to your father and get the first flight home. Mr Birthistle will go free, but there is nothing we can do about that.'

'But can't you have him arrested … stopped?' Fintan was genuinely shocked.

'How? On what evidence? On the basis of a *dream* you had in a plane, 50,000 feet above Africa? Sorry Fintan, but there will not be a jot of evidence against him. The only evidence we have is this actual mine here. You and your father would be arrested, not Birthistle. You would end up in prison here and we would have an international incident on our hands, perhaps even the civil war that Birthistle plans with Murabende.'

'But can't I get evidence, rifle his luggage or something?'

'You weren't listening. He will have nothing, not so much as an address book!'

'Please Mr Eriksen, I'll get evidence! I'll get him drunk. He gets very talkative with me when we're alone and he's drunk, and you can listen.'

Yola sensed the desperation in his voice. To her surprise, Hans hesitated.

'I'm his blue-eyed boy,' Fintan urged. 'He wants me to marry his daughter!'

Yola's lips tightened, but Hans said, 'I cannot get involved. We are a neutral organisation. But I'd like to hear what he has to say. My name is not on this walkman, could you carry this?'

'No, he's a patter, you know, little pats and pushes, all very matey, he'd notice a recorder at once.'

Yola could hear bangs and shouts outside as the deminers returned from their work on the bridge. It was four o'clock. There wasn't much time left.

'I could go!' said Yola suddenly. 'I'm Kasemban, he wouldn't notice me.'

'I'm not so sure about that,' said Hans.

'No, Hans,' she said, 'I mean it. I've only been in the hotel once, but there are rooms and alcoves off the bar. If Fintan can get him into one of those, I think I know how I can get close enough to hear and record what they say. But I will need the walkman, and I will need Judit's help.'

Hans looked at her suspiciously. Fintan opened the walkman, popped the tape into his shirt pocket and handed the recorder to Yola.

'Well, first things first, let's get Fintan down to the hotel. Fintan, we'll talk on the way. Judit, can you bring Yola down later? And take care of that walkman, it's special.' Hans turned, but the two girls already had their heads together. He shrugged.

'Look for me in the foyer, Fintan,' Yola called. 'Tell me where you are, but don't expect a reply – remember, I don't speak English.'

'I'll be ready,' Fintan nodded.

20

Good Time Girl

'Judit – Judit stop, it's European lipstick, it will look ... mmm.' Yola's protest ended in a mumble as the Dutch girl, holding her firmly by the chin, started to apply a thick coat of lipstick.

'Relax, don't smile, it makes your lips go thin. We must make you look voluptuous!'

Yola had no idea what voluptuous meant, but it seemed just the right word to describe their last crazy half-hour.

She was remembering the only time she'd been inside the Palace Hotel. Uncle Banda had taken her in, just to have a look. Most Kasembans could not afford to go in there because one drink alone cost a day's wages. The only Kasemban women there were the wives of government officials and strange, solitary girls extravagantly dressed, smoking alone at small tables.

'Don't stare!' Uncle Banda had whispered. 'Those are good time girls.'

'What are good time girls?' she'd asked.

'Girls who hope some rich man will buy them a drink or take them to the disco.'

When Yola got upstairs, Judit already had her small wardrobe thrown out on the bed. Yola made a dart for a bright print, but Judit took it from her.

'No, you are a good time girl, you must wear black,' and she held a long black tube dress up against a startled Yola. Helpless, in that no man's land between horror and giggles, Yola let herself be peeled like a banana and then, in an attitude of surrender, inserted into Judit's black tube dress. The fit was surprisingly good, but Judit wasn't satisfied.

'You are the wrong shape for the job!' she complained. 'What we need is more bosom.'

Once again, Yola's vocabulary let her down, however when she understood what Judit meant their whole scheme nearly foundered in uncontrollable laughter.

Eventually she stood in front of the mirror, truly startled at the transformation before her. All that she had ever wanted, and more! She turned to Judit, intending to give her a hug, but found that when it came to moving, her feet seemed to be tied together. She felt like a goat with its legs hobbled. The black dress might be perfect for a girl with two sound limbs, but for an amputee it was a disaster. Judit grabbed her scissors.

'You can't!' Yola exclaimed, seeing Judit on her knees.

'This is your good leg, isn't it?'

'Ouch. Yes.'

'Well, you are going to show a lot of it!'

'But your beautiful dress!'

'Don't worry, it will just be the seam.'

Judit stepped back to view her work. Yola walked over to the mirror and the black dress parted seductively up her thigh. Her artificial leg was concealed. They were impressed, and a little awed by their success.

'I have an evening bag you could put Hans's walkman in. I reckon you should wear the earphones, it will make Mr Birthistle think you can't hear. More like you're waiting for someone.'

'Oh Judit, I can't. You don't think someone will want me to dance? I *can't*!'

Judit laughed. 'I wouldn't be surprised at all. But I'll be there to keep an eye on you.'

◆   ◇   ◆

Judit's small car climbed laboriously in and out of the gigantic ruts on the road down to the hotel. Twice, Yola opened her mouth to ask her to forget the whole escapade, but she was stopped each time by the thought of the desperation in Fintan's voice. They had a moment of panic when Yola, practising with the controls of Hans's walkman, discovered that he had forgotten to put a blank tape in it. Then Judit had the bright idea of covering the broken-out tabs of a music cassette, which she had in the car, with postage stamps; it recorded perfectly.

◆   ◇   ◆

Standing outside the Nopani Palace Hotel, Yola looked longingly after Judit's homely little car as it lurched towards the car park. She had never felt so alone. Her unnatural bosom caught her eye as she looked down to walk, and the slit in her dress seemed to stretch up to her armpit. A mixed group of Kasembans and Europeans approached, making for the revolving door of the hotel. Yola followed closely – anything to get over this first hurdle. One of the European men stood back to let her into the door ahead of him. Before she could stop him he had crowded into the segment of the door beside her. For a horrifying moment she felt a hand on her thigh. She was furious and made to hit him but there wasn't room, all she managed was a seductive movement of her padded chest against him. She heard jeers from his watching companions, who pushed on the door and ejected her like a pip from an orange into the entrance hall.

Gathering her wits and her dignity, Yola thrust through the leering faces and made for the foyer. The one thing she wanted was a mirror to see if anything was out of place. She turned into an alcove and was met by a girl looking anxiously for something. With a start, she realised that it was her own reflection; the alcove was backed by a mirror! She apologised automatically and backed away. She looked down to check her dress, and noticed that she had almost walked into an arrangement of dead flowers in the alcove. But all was well. Her outfit was fine, and the flowers hadn't fallen over. She turned and surveyed the room, it was full but not crowded. She chose a small table with a view into the bar and sat down; her skirt parted in an alarming manner but she dared not touch it because heads were turning.

She had never been the centre of attention like this. The women's heads turned with sharp disapproval. Men's eyes swivelled in barely concealed appreciation. At a table nearby a group of middle-aged aid workers tried not to notice her. One had a small silver cross around her neck: a nun. What if Sister Martha came in? Another minute and Yola would have walked out, but then she looked towards the bar. There was Fintan, staring at her as if he had seen a ghost. She smiled with relief and, without thinking, beckoned him with her head. The faces, which till then had been concentrating on her, swivelled towards Fintan. Face flaming scarlet he crossed the room and leant down. Turning his eyes from her exposed thigh he whispered, 'We're in the small room directly over from the bar! Please God, I can keep a straight face.'

Yola tossed her head and told him to get lost in Kasembi, then she took out the earphones of her walkman and pressed the record button. She waited till he had disappeared and then got up in a leisurely manner and followed him across the room.

✦　✧　✦

There was no sign of Fintan or anyone else in the small room. She sat down out of sight of the door and took up a magazine, hoping that she had got the right room. A waiter appeared with a tray. Speaking firmly in Kasembi, she ordered bottled water with lemon and ice. Judit had told her that this would look like gin and tonic. It cost her a day's wages for the drink, so she tipped the waiter with another day's wages and a smile in the hope that he would leave her alone. She glanced at the magazine, but apart from wondering at the name, OHM, could not focus on it. Suddenly she realised that someone had come in and was standing behind her. A man's voice, magnified in her earphones, said in English, 'Scuse me Miss, this room's taken.'

She smiled up at him, shrugged helplessly and told him in Kasembi that she did not understand. He gazed down, swaying slightly, and asked her where she was from, but his words were slurred so she had no difficulty shrugging again and managing to show a bit more thigh. He patted her on the shoulder. Then, to her alarm, reached down towards her lap. She shrank back, but all he did was take the magazine she was holding and turn it the other way up. As he moved away she heard him say, 'Seems to speak no English, and I suspect she can't even read. If it wasn't for Becky, I'd say you should try your luck, eh lad!'

Fintan's reply came with unnecessary vigour. 'No thanks! Not my type at all.'

Yola struggled to suppress a grin and stared at the magazine as if her fortune were written in it. That man must have been Mr Birthistle. Then she realised why he had turned the magazine around for her – WHO magazine, of course!

✦ ✧ ✦

They seemed to be taking up a conversation they had started before.

'Well done lad, good answer, I'll let you pick up a chance card for that.'

Yola was alert – surely this was Birthistle's arms-game talk! How had Fintan got him started on that? She forced herself to turn a page of her magazine; her fingers were sticky with sweat. Then she realised she had missed Fintan's reply.

'Nukes, boy? No, no, no. Don't touch them, put that card back.' It was so realistic that Yola was tempted to turn to see if they really had cards. 'Tell you why?' Mr Birthistle continued. 'Simple, I don't want my Becky nuked, and the only people that'd buy an atom bomb would nuke just about anybody. Myself, I don't mind the anti-nuclear campaign because while they march they take people's minds off our little business. Who'd bother about banning a machine-gun when they could ban an atom bomb! Let's throw the dice again.'

'How about this?' laughed Fintan. 'Pretend I've landed on a square that says Dublin Conference on Arms Control – it starts in a few days – should I buy that?'

'Ha ha, Fintan old son! You want to know what will happen if your Dad has a change of heart, don't you. Crafty, I like you! You're like me, you know, two peas in a pod, and you just starting out in life. Makes me feel young to help you. Well … let me see … that conference could be bad news for the toy trade so … how about this. Let's say I had a little project in Africa, for example, exporting air bag stabilisers to the natives. Suddenly my partner tries to pull out, all that effort, all that money down the drain – all can I do is bring Plan B into operation. Imagine it,' here Mr Birthistle's voice acquired a dramatic turn, 'it's the first day of the Dublin conference. Everyone is patting little neutral Ireland on the back, cetra, cetra, then up speaks a voice. "Madam President. Do you know that Ireland is making a particularly nasty landmine designed to kill deminers? Here is the evidence!" Gasp – hush – horror. Talk your way out of that, Madam President!'

'But you'd be caught!' Fintan sounded genuinely shocked.

'Don't worry lad, it's your dad who'd be caught, hooked and landed, not me. I'm just the agent for a motor company. Look in my briefcase, not a shred of evidence. Anyway, I wouldn't do it.'

'Why … why not?'

''Cos I like you lad, marry you off to Becky. Think about it, I'll teach you all you need to know. But I need to shed a tear now. Old age. Keep my drink warm for me.'

Yola didn't dare turn, but Fintan was beside her in a second.

'I can't go on, Yola. He's going to trip me up and I'll wreck everything. We're caught, aren't we? Dad must have signed up, and if Birthistle blows the Dublin conference, Dad will go to jail."

'Nonsense, you're doing great! This is the first evidence he's given away and it's all on tape! And Fintan, he sounds lonely, work on it.'

'Hush, he's coming!'

'Eh … eh … you leave that black cookie alone.' The voice was so close, Yola was sure he must have heard them talking. 'What *is* she doing here anyway? I'm …'

At that moment the walkman clicked off. The tape had run out. Yola didn't know what to do. She must turn the tape over, but she knew he was watching her. She opened Judit's bag; her hands were shaking. She extracted the walkman and began to turn the tape. All at once there was a sharp tap on her shoulder. She thrust the tape down hastily; the wretched postage stamps stood out like beacons. She turned and Mr Birthistle's face was only inches from her own. His smile was half menace, half humour as he pointed to her earphones as if he wanted to listen.

The waft of alcohol from his breath almost choked her. She passed him one of her tiny earphones and watched him press it into the forest of ginger hair growing out of his ear. Her finger hovered over the play button, but panic swept over her: had she turned the tape or just pushed it back in without turning it? What if he heard his own voice? The hiss as the tape-leader wound through seemed to last forever. Then, with a crash that made them both jump, Judit's favourite Zairian band burst out. Yola jigged nervously with the music, then she gave the sweaty white man beside her a cheeky look and flicked the earphone from his ear. He tickled her under the chin and returned to Fintan. She waited a tense moment or two and then pressed record again. Birthistle was talking, he seemed relaxed and the charm she had noticed earlier was back.

'Look old boy, I've no son, made a bit of money, house in England, office in Ostend, but it's getting towards the time I settled down. I need someone bright like you, not too squeamish either. Interested?'

'Well ... it depends, tell me ...'

'Ok, scored again Fintan! Pass Go and double your money! Always be careful. So, you want info, here's info.'

Birthistle's voice was thickening but his mind seemed clear. Yola sat riveted, she couldn't believe it, sometimes he reverted to arms-game talk, but at other times he was naming names: dealers, companies and clients. When the tape eventually clicked off, Yola realised that they had enough evidence to hang the man twice over. She leant back, closed her eyes and relaxed, her skirt slipped further off her thigh.

'Jeepers, look at the time.' That was Fintan.

'That's right, beauty sleep for the wicked. I'll phone Becky that you were asking after her?'

'Er yes, yes, please do!' Yola ground her teeth. 'Good night.'

Silence. Fintan had gone, but had Birthistle? Yola didn't dare turn. She felt rather than saw the arms dealer come over and looked up. He was looking down at her with what she could only think of as a leer. She fought back panic and forced herself to take her time. She took off her earphones and coiled them down on the walkman; he mustn't become suspicious of that. Then she looked up and smiled as if she had known he would come. His watery eyes were exploring her exposed thigh. Suddenly all the hate she had bottled up during the evening exploded. To hell with the tape, to hell with it all! Feast your eyes on this! she said to herself. With a seductiveness that she didn't know she possessed, she slid her dress clean off both knees. Mr Birthistle's eyes seemed to swell in their sockets. Then he noticed her artificial leg. Good though it was, even he couldn't miss it. He stepped back, gulping.

'Oh God, oh God, I think I'm going to be sick!' He lunged towards the door but it was already open, he didn't see it and walked straight into its sharp edge.

Yola twisted the gaping skirt tight about her legs and dropped her head into her hands. When Fintan came in it was like a rush of wind and he was kneeling, holding onto her.

'Are you all right? What did he do?'

Feelings of triumph, revulsion and bitter sweetness flowed through her. Birthistle reeling and crashing against the door was worth a lot, but had it been worth that awful pawing leer, this feeling of being dirty? She wanted to throw her arms about Fintan, to ruffle his hair, but she couldn't now; she felt unclean.

'Fintan, your Dad?'

'I know, I know, I've got to see him. But I had to see if you were all right.'

'I just feel dirty.'

21

Gabbin Needs You

Fintan was holding Yola's hand as they emerged into the foyer, but he relinquished it as Hans and Judit came towards them. The foyer was nearly empty now.

'Where did Birthistle go?' Fintan asked.

'Upstairs to bed, I imagine,' Hans said. 'Where's your dad?'

'Oh God, we're not finished yet are we?' A look of pain crossed Fintan's face. 'I told him what I had found out, and I left him looking at a pile of your landmines literature and the video of the operation Yola and I saw on that poor girl in the hospital yesterday. I'm afraid all his dreams have been shattered. I'll go now.'

But Fintan did not go, because at that moment the swing doors at the foot of the stairs burst open, there was an enraged shout and Mr Birthistle backed into the room, waving his arms in a mixture of surrender and defence as a smaller and older version of Fintan advanced on him. Mr O'Farrell was in a towering rage, shouting and thrusting at the startled arms dealer. Blind to where they were going, Mr Birthistle was being backed into the alcove with the mirror that Yola had found earlier. His feet came up against the flowerpot, he toppled back and crumpled up against the mirror. Mr O'Farrell, thwarted by his fall, stood glaring at the heaving mass of dead flowers and waving legs.

'Dad!' Fintan called. 'Over here!'

'Come on,' Judit said quickly to Yola, 'let's get this good time girl into the ladies and wash some of her warpaint off.'

✦ ✧ ✦

It was a very sober group that sat in the deserted bar later. Mr O'Farrell glared at the table as if his gaze could burn a hole in it. His eyes flickered up and saw Yola watching him, a grim little smile flashed and he was gone. Hans took the walkman from her; they fell silent. He tipped out the cassette and carefully prised off the postage stamps so the tape could not be recorded on again by mistake.

'This is as unnerving as defusing a mine,' he said grimly. Then he put the tape back into the walkman and pressed rewind for what seemed an age. 'Now for it!'

They all leant forward as he pressed the play button, they heard ... nothing ... not even a hiss. What had gone wrong? Was there nothing on the tape? Had the microphone become detached? Yola nearly cried ... then she remembered!

'Volume, Hans,' she gasped, 'I turned it down, it's on the top.'

Hans span the small wheel. There, against the recorded rustle of Yola's movements and the rapid patter of her heartbeat, was Birthistle's voice. '... anything, boy, from peashooters to rocket launchers, M60s to tanks ...' There was a muted cheer from the gathering. Hands patted Yola on the back. They listened to the tape, but she had heard it all and dropped off asleep out of sheer exhaustion.

She woke to hear Mr O'Farrell saying, 'My one regret is that he fell over that bloody flowerpot before I could hit him. You see all our talk in Murabende was technical. How to record

166

particular sound patterns and transfer them on to the chip –
they knew their stuff. That idiot Birthistle was just a nuisance,
with his nodding and winking. I just said, yes, yes, yes – it's the
only way to quieten him, you know. In the end they got tired of
him too and sent him off to the bar to get drunk. Look, can't
we just turn him over to the Kasemban authorities?'

'I'm afraid he's not the idiot he looks,' Hans replied. 'You
can be sure that he is clean of anything incriminating. It is you
he fooled and you who is carrying all the evidence.'

'He fooled me because I didn't want to know. Fintan said it,
but I wouldn't listen to him. But ... I'm not carrying much evidence now. I left the six prototypes we brought in Murabende,
and they only had test data on them.'

'Do you realise what that test data is?'

'No. It was just test sounds, bleeps and clicks and whines, all
quite meaningless.'

'No, Mr O'Farrell, not meaningless. Those are the recorded
sounds of every known mine detector in the world, possibly.
Those six 'prototypes' are enough to stop our work completely. How can I put my men into a minefield knowing that
one of these may blow up in his face?'

'Well, I must try to get them back ... I'll claim they need
technical modification or something. They seemed reasonable
people.'

'Ya, ya sure!' Hans was sarcastic. 'They have wives and nice
kids at expensive boarding schools. They perhaps think they
do something good, ya? But I say they are more evil than any
African that ever pulled a trigger. They will know that you
have turned against them and will either get you arrested or
kill you Mr O'Farrell, they are not *reasonable people*!'

Yola had never seen Hans really angry before. Mr O'Farrell
didn't wilt, as she would have done, but asked, 'Should I go to

the police here, then?'

'No. Go. Go home now. If you stay around here you will either rot in prison, where you will be no good to anyone, or you will start an international incident – and in Africa that's as good an excuse as any to start a war. The best thing you can do is take this tape – I will make a copy – and get home ahead of this Birthistle. There is enough on this to interest any police force, Interpol in particular. Get him stopped if you can, because his threat to the Dublin peace conference is real. The arms trade hates that conference and they'd give real money for proof that Ireland, the host country, is manufacturing landmines. My God, don't you realise? Ireland was one of the first countries to sign the ban! Birthistle has probably already been paid for bringing you over here. Since you backed him into that flowerpot he knows this project is over, so why not make some dollars selling the story to the rivals.'

Mr O'Farrell nodded. 'Ok, we'll go,' he said. 'How can we get out of here ahead of him?'

Yola looked at Fintan; she hadn't thought that he would have to go immediately. She managed a smile. He was looking at her, but his lips just narrowed. Hans was looking at his watch.

'Let me see, the only flight out of Nopani tomorrow morning is one for relief workers, he won't be allowed on that. If I can get you and Fintan on to that flight it will give you a head start. Go, pack, and get some rest, that flight leaves at eight.'

Yola stood disconsolately while everyone milled around. Fintan came up to her. And she said, 'I won't see you again.'

'Yes you will if you get up early. Hans is going to copy the tape. We'll pick it up on our way to the airport. I wish I wasn't going now. I feel I should be trying to get those mines back, not running away.'

'Back from Murabende? You must be joking! But I'll come with you and see you off.'

✦ ◇ ✦

Yola lay on her bed; she undid the valve on her leg but did not remove it. She didn't want to be struggling to bandage her stump when the taxi came. She was exhausted, but strangely elated. She knew she would never get to sleep and so was surprised when Judit shook her and said, 'Yola, wake up! The car's come, don't you want to see Fintan off?' Yola was so deep in sleep that she might as well have been drowning. Judit slapped and cajoled as if she too realised that this should be an important moment for Yola.

The taxi stood silently in front of the office, not wasting petrol. Hans was talking to Mr O'Farrell through the front window. Fintan was standing at the back door. He was waiting for her to come and her heart was doing strange things inside her chest. She started towards the car, but at that moment a figure rose from the watchman's chair in front of the office.

'Ehee, Yola!' it called softly, 'I've been waiting for you.'

'Shimima – I see you,' called Yola, but she was deeply confused. Why was Shimima here?

'Yola, little sister, I have a message for you from Senior Mother.'

Yola's heart sank. 'Oh Shimima, can't it wait? I want to go to the airport.'

'Listen to the message, little one. Your Uncle Banda is returned. Gabbin is in trouble.'

'Gabbin!' Yola repeated. She looked desperately from Shimima to Fintan and back. She had to make a choice. She might never see … At this moment it meant everything to her to see Fintan off. She took a deep breath.

'Fintan,' she said, 'I've … Shimima here tells me … Gabbin

169

my … the boy who saved my life needs me … I must go to look for him.' How could she make him understand?

When he answered it was with a slightly sad smile; he was very like his father. 'Don't worry, I know all about Gabbin, Catherine told me about him. Of course you must go.'

Yola stepped forward and put her arms around him briefly, but it was a formal embrace. They watched the taxi disappear, then Shimima took her hand and Yola buried her face in her shoulder.

'I'm proud of you, little sister,' her friend whispered.

He's been waiting all along, hasn't he, like one of King Arthur's bloody knights waiting for the trump to sound! And I had begun to think that 'Gabbin' was part of Catherine's imagination. Gabbin – it seeems a small name for a six-foot warrior. He clearly means a lot to her though. Hans wants us gone. We've messed up enough here. It's time to go. We touch down in Simbada shortly.

22

The Child Soldier

Standing in the doorway, Yola surveyed the scene in Father's room. Father was sitting formally in his great chair; his fly-switch lay on a small table to his right. Senior Mother hovered darkly behind his left shoulder. Uncle Banda sat skewed, half collapsed on a three-legged stool with his back to her. Father looked up.

'Get out! This is a matter for Senior Mother only.'

Yola was taken aback. 'Father, it is me, Yola. I thought I was called?'

Senior Mother bent forward and whispered in his ear. Father took his time, she could feel his mind reaching out for hers.

'You may come in. Stand beside your Uncle Banda.' He touched his fly-switch; it was a command. As she advanced, Uncle Banda seemed to shrink still deeper into himself.

'Banda, in another time my daughter, Yola, had a special friend in your godson, Gabbin.' Yola noticed the deep irony in her father's voice as he said the word 'godson'. 'Now I am going to ask you the question you have avoided answering for me so far. Is the boy dead?'

Yola bit her lip. Uncle Banda stiffened for a moment, began to say yes, then dropped his voice and in a despairing whisper said, 'I don't know!'

✦ ✧ ✦

Yola listened while Father took Uncle Banda back over a story he had clearly told once before. Father was in pursuit of details, while she was trying to piece the story together from fragments. There was a lull in the questions and suddenly Uncle Banda became aware of her standing beside him. He took her hand and began to caress it absently. His hands were cold.

'As a boy I always wanted to be a soldier, Yola,' he said in a low voice. 'I watched the government troops, but they always seemed to be doing nothing or something boring. Then one day the rebels passed through our village. They came silently in combat gear, got food and water and were gone. Some of them were no older than me, and I was only ten. They told us about their cause and handed us leaflets with pictures, freedom from communism it was in those days, but to me it could have been anything with a long name. It was the excitement that got me. From then on, whenever fighting broke out I was part of it. I was with the KLA during the civil war, we lost, but we felt we were honourable. When it was over, your Father here was kind and took me back into our family. But I still felt an outcast here in the compound – I longed to have a cause again and to be off in the night, just to kill boredom. While you were away, Gabbin and me got on fine. He's my godson, so I had a right. We were alive together. I wanted him to know what it is like to have companions and to share in a great idea. He is bright and clever and I knew he'd enjoy the danger and having friends, also I thought the training would be good for him, so …'

'Tell her what sort of training you mean! It wasn't school-work? It wasn't training in wisdom, was it? It wasn't how to herd cattle or plant crops?' interjected Father harshly.

'Yola, believe me, I didn't think it would turn out as it did. There are … there were those of us who still felt we had an honourable cause. We wanted our young men to know what it is like to believe in something beyond themselves. We made a camp in the Noose, where the rebels are training again. We taught them how to carry messages, how to use a radio, how to scout and how to hide.'

'Who?' Father demanded. 'Tell Yola about your "young men". Do not lie, Banda, with half-truths. These are children, *our* children. They are not young men, they are child soldiers, just as you still are.'

Something in her father's voice made Yola look up. He had taken up his fly-switch and was lashing it back and forth like the tail of a lion before its charge. Something frightening was happening. Uncle Banda seemed locked in silence, his breath was coming heavily. Then, with terrible certainty, Yola realised that Father was, even now, deep in her Uncle Banda's mind, just as he had got into hers at the time of her trial.

Uncle Banda was pulling down on her hand like a heavy weight. She struggled to pull away. Her mind shrieked out for help. Did Father know? She was being pulled down and down through the turmoil of their battling minds. Then, there was silence; she had sunk below the waves, she was in another place and in another time.

Tall trees towered above her. Under one of these sat a small boy, happily oiling and caressing his rifle. The dappled light on his camouflage fatigues made him difficult to see.

'Gabbin!' she called, but he didn't hear her. She shifted position slightly. No, it wasn't Gabbin, it was – of course – it was the little Banda. He looked so innocent in his quiet enjoyment. There was a crash among the bushes a little way ahead. In a trice the boy had rolled off the path, cocked his rifle and was aiming down the path.

'*Don't!*' she called, but of course he didn't hear her. Then she experienced his terror. The boots of the man pounded the forest floor, he grew larger and larger; the little boy raised his rifle. Yola screamed as Father wrenched her mind back from the abyss, but he was too late to save her entirely – the sensations that the child Banda had experienced lingered like the smell of death in her mind.

Father held her mind firmly, and she sobbed and shook while the visions of what she had seen dulled. She could see it all: it was a trap, a gruesome cycle of violence supported by an empty dream. The child soldier grew into an adult, but with a child's mind. Father had let her see the unspeakable.

As Yola came back into the present she felt Uncle Banda's grip on her hand loosen. Rage welled up inside her until it consumed her completely. This was what Banda had been doing to Gabbin – her Gabbin! She lurched around so that she was facing him; her back was to Father. His eyes squirmed away from her. She raised her hand deliberately and slapped him as hard as she could across the face. His head jolted to one side; she hit him again. Then she turned to Senior Mother and Father to take her punishment; her head drooped and her anger was spent. Senior Mother nodded; Father touched his fly-switch – he approved of what she had done.

'Your uncle has a wound, Yola. Tend to it.'

They were dismissed.

✦　✧　✦

'Where is he, Uncle Banda?' she asked as she washed his wounds. Two holes: the bullet had gone cleanly through.

'The Noose, the Hangman's Noose.'

'How did you get in there? There are hundreds of people who want to return to their land there but can't because of the landmines. How did you get in?'

'There is a way through the minefield, but it is guarded.

There is a training camp for adults there. Food and guns come across the river from Murabende.'

'And the children?'

'They are orphans, abused kids, street kids, we gave them food, shelter, something to live for. Gabbin was a star!'

'Of course Gabbin was a star!' snapped Yola. Poor Gabbin, he would have loved it until ... 'What went wrong? Why are you here?' She reached for a bandage.

'It all changed.' A chill seemed to seep into the room; Uncle Banda shivered.

'How?'

'A team of instructors came in from the advanced training camps in Murabende – white mercenaries for the adults and a so-called child soldier expert for the kids, the bastard!' Uncle Banda shook his head. 'It wasn't necessary, they were good kids but this ... this ... expert, he said they needed to be blooded.'

Yola felt sick. 'Blooded?'

Uncle Banda nodded and swallowed painfully. 'Taught to fight hand to hand, even to kill.' His voice wobbled. He cleared his throat to get it under control. 'One of the instructors would pick on one of the weaker boys for punishment by the others. Gradually the punishments got worse and worse. I argued, but I was afraid it could make things bad for Gabbin. He was still the star pupil and had managed to avoid having anything to do with the beatings. The expert noticed this in the end. It was time for Gabbin's pride to be pricked. They knew I was his godfather and they knew I hated their methods, so they denounced me, tried me and condemned me to be shot. The boy chosen to shoot me was Gabbin.

'The boys who tied me up did so loosely; they risked their lives in doing that. Gabbin had no choice; the instructor had a gun to his head as he aimed. They stood me beside the river – no graves for traitors. I decided that, hit or not, I would pretend that I had been. The whole class had to shout, "Three, two, one", it was that that gave me warning. The instructor could see if Gabbin aimed more than inches wide. I put on a good act. Poor Gabbin, he aimed to miss but he probably thinks he killed me. I was face down in the river when the instructor decided to finish me off; he missed, but put this bullet through my leg.'

'How's the camp organised?' demanded Yola.

'It is the boys who guard the minefield. Two shifts, changing at midnight. They say that they are training them not to be afraid of the dark, in fact it's just so the grown soldiers can sleep and drink in peace. There is little danger. There is no way through the minefield because the mines are re-laid after each crossing. And now they have a special mine that blows up when a mine detector crosses over it.'

Yola looked up sharply; they'd only just got the mines, why so quickly? she wondered. But then Uncle Banda provided the answer.

'The rebels are afraid the Kasemban army may try to force a way through the minefield today. You see, the adult soldiers are away on exercise at the moment.'

'How did you get out?' asked Yola.

'Swam down river.'

'But crocodiles!?' she shivered.

'They must have been asleep. I had no choice. The men will be back tomorrow, I couldn't hang about, not with a bullet in the leg.'

Yola, who had a safety pin in her mouth, nodded. Then something he had said struck her. Her bandaging slowed, what was that he had said about the soldiers being away?

'Where are they – the rebel soldiers? Who's in the Noose now?' The safety pin slipped from her mouth.

'The boys and their instructors, of course. The men are in Murabende on a big exercise with the army there, that's why they put in the new mines, it was an added protection.'

'How many instructors?'

'Three – now that I've gone that is. Time for them to get drunk. With the senior officers away it will be party time. Gabbin and his lads will be in sole charge of the first shift to-night.' Uncle Banda put a hand on Yola's arm. 'If we could get mine detectors ... No, I'd forgotten, there's this new mine ...'

Yola stood looking down at her uncle slumped in the chair. He'd been rough with her, but always fair. When she spoke, she spoke quietly so that she could gauge his trustworthiness.

'Uncle Banda, whose side are you on?'

To her surprise he took her hand, as he had earlier. 'Yola, you have never had Chief Abonda dig through your mind, tear you apart, turn you inside out to show you the inner, yellow part of you! I brought Gabbin into all this. I would walk through the middle of that minefield alone to rescue him now, but all the good that that would do would be to find the first mine.'

She groped for the safety pin she had dropped and slipped it in at a low angle into the bandage. 'Uncle Banda, there is a door to that minefield and I think I'm the only one who can open it.'

Slowly, thinking it out step by step, she explained, questioning him for details on how the boy soldiers operated, and who would be where and when. Uncle Banda said little, but as her plan developed she could feel his enthusiasm mounting. It was like a vibration between them. No wonder Gabbin had followed him. When she finished, his eyes were focussed somewhere far beyond where they were sitting.

Suddenly she had a last misgiving.

'Uncle Banda,' she said, 'tell me, we are not playing child soldiers, are we?'

He did her the justice of pausing while he thought. He put his hand up to his cheek. 'You know Yola, you hit me very hard!' He wasn't teasing her; he was thanking her. 'The child soldier in me died with that slap, and you will never be one.'

◆ ◇ ◆

Yola told Senior Mother that she had to return to work and that Uncle Banda would come with her to see if he could get news of Gabbin. They got a taxi into town together. It was a minibus and it had so many people hanging out of it by the end that it looked like a bunch of grapes. Yola sat on Banda's knee while the driver shouted the news.

'Did you hear? The Kasemban army tried to get through the minefield into the Noose last night?' he roared. 'What do they think they are doing … risking war with Murabende. That place has a spell on it! There is bad medicine about … two deminers injured … *two*! They are saying now there are mines that can smell them coming. I reckon it's the soldier's feet. Ever smelled a soldier's feet! Blew up in their faces they did. Now the deminers are refusing to go in there.'

They were not far from the NPA camp when Uncle Banda said, 'Let us down here, please.' He helped Yola out.

'Where are you going now?' Yola asked.

'Don't ask child, just get all the rest you can. If you can get us past those new mines then—'

But Yola interrupted. 'No Uncle, what are you planning? We are going to rescue Gabbin – nothing more!'

Banda shook his head. 'If we find Gabbin you can go, but you weren't there when your father took my mind and showed me—'

'Oh yes I was! And it was you that dragged me there!'

Her uncle flinched. 'I'm sorry Yola, but you see why I must do something to stop this thing.'

'What thing?'

'War is about to start again. The KLA is not dead. For the last year weapons have been brought quietly across the river into the Noose lands. There are enough stored there now for a major attack. The plan is simple: a special force will cross the river from Murabende, pick up their weapons in the Noose, slip out through the minefield and seize the bridges from this side. KLA artillery and equipment can then cross from Murabende. Within a day we – I mean, they – could have control of Nopani again.'

'Not again! Haven't we had enough war? Is there nothing we can do?'

'I don't know Yola, but for the first time in my life I seem to be trying to stop a war instead of start one. I just hope people will trust me. Be at the place I said at sundown, ok?'

Yola watched her uncle limp away and fought back her bitterness against him. What had he to lose? When she turned she could see the gates to the deminers' camp in the distance. What she was doing was betrayal. Time and again Hans had told her that they were a neutral peace-keeping organisation and couldn't get involved in political acts, no matter how worthy and justified. No country would have them if they did. She would have to leave the NPA and that meant losing everything she had lived and worked for since that day Hans's Landcruiser had first driven past the compound.

She turned in at the gate of the camp and a huge lump grew in her throat. She'd been so proud of working with everyone here. She'd shared Hans's pride when they'd put up the Northern People's Aid sign at the gate. She loved the work. He'd done so much for her, and she couldn't even explain. When she got to the adjutant's house she couldn't resist walking quietly down the corridor to listen outside Hans's office. She heard the phone being slammed down. Then she heard him talking to Judit.

'Damn them! Damn them! That was the army colonel on the phone. It was his men that were injured yesterday. I can't believe that they got those mines ready to lay so quickly! They must be the mines that that fool O'Farrell left in Murabende. They say they went off directly under the mine detectors. I can't even offer the colonel help because this is an international dispute. I can just see the headlines: 'NPA Takes Sides in Border Dispute with Murabende!' Anyway, how can I send my own men out with mine detectors now! There were six mines left in Murabende, weren't there Judit? Now there are only four. Until the last one is found our work is crippled!'

Yola backed away from the door and retreated as quietly as she could. She climbed the stairs to her room, closed the door and began to pack. She carefully separated anything that was not hers, even the NPA T-shirt she was so proud of, and put these in a pile to leave behind on her bed. Her few personal possessions she put into her suitcase. Then she sat down to write a letter. It took several drafts.

To Mr Hans Eriksen, Northern People's Aid, Nopani.
Dear Sir,
I am sorry that I resign my job as Trainee Mines Awareness Instructor today.
With many thanks for kind help.
Sincerely,
Yola Abonda.
P.S. I have given dog Sailor one day leave. Y.

Her next note was to Judit, asking her to give Hans's letter to him in the morning and to look after her suitcase till she could collect it. She thought for a minute and then explained, very briefly, what she was planning to do. She knew she could trust Judit and ... well, if things went wrong, Judit would tell Hans. It was important to her that Hans should not think badly of her. She cried a bit, then she slept.

At dusk, Yola absconded with Sailor and joined a silent group waiting for transport at the appointed place. Some she recognised as NPA men, many of whom were from the Noose, but they too were incognito; there wasn't a uniform among them. Uncle Banda had certainly got the word around. One by one, the stars began to prick the canopy of night above.

23

The Long Night

Waves of sheer terror at the enormity of what she had started swept over Yola. She could hear nothing, she could see nothing – but the night was charged with unseen energy. She stared at the faint luminescence above the forest. Would the moon never rise? Perhaps it wouldn't and they could all go home. Sailor whined softly at her feet. The people were somewhere behind her, the people of the Noose, like ghosts exiled from a haunted land waiting to be exorcised, waiting to return to their land. Despite the crowded night, she felt utterly alone. Someone laughed in the dark and then stifled it. A plane passed high overhead, a silent winking light among the stars. She thought of Fintan, her mind told her he was up there somewhere, an unconstant star winking its way out of her life, but in her heart she felt him near. She thought of Gabbin, as he used to be, the pink flash of his feet as he ran. How much had he changed? Was he even alive? A car sounding like Judit's puttered past on the road, stopped and then returned the way it had come. A cow lowed – surely they weren't bringing their cattle? A sigh like the end of a long-held breath flowed from the invisible gathering. She turned; a first sliver of the moon's rim was rising, silver above the black cut-out of the forest. It was time to move. There were steps behind her. Sailor whined with pleasure and a familiar voice said 'Yola?' and the night changed for her.

✦ ✧ ✦

Fintan looked pale in the moonlight beside her Uncle Banda.

'I knew you were near,' she said.

He stepped forward; the moon, flooding ever stronger, picked out lines of tiredness etched in his face.

'I had to come, Yola. The news about the soldiers being injured by our mines was just breaking when we got to Simbada. I wanted to run, go with Father, but I couldn't. I thought about you, searching for your friend; I thought about those mines waiting in the ground. I must at least try to find them before someone else is killed or injured. Father understood, he gave me money and I got the relief flight back; Judit brought me down. I want to be with you, I want to help you if I can. If you're ready, let's go and find your friend.'

He stood looking at her, his formal speech over, waiting to see if he were welcome. Emotions sparked and criss-crossed inside her. She was hearing his words, but she was also hearing something about his feelings for her. She turned to look at the moon. It finally broke free from the forest rim and seemed to leap into the sky. The turmoil inside her calmed. She was ready; the missing piece of the jigsaw had been found. It needed recognition, nothing more. She turned and put her arms out and held him hard and close for a moment.

✦ ✧ ✦

The men came forward and took up their positions. One of them laid a tape along the path that bordered the minefield. Two others were ready to unroll similar tapes to mark the left and right limits of Sailor's figure of eight loops. Yola handed a bundle of weighted cloth markers to Fintan.

'I need someone who isn't afraid of Sailor to mark any mines we find. You've seen me do it. I'll have to control Sailor, there won't be room to throw his bear out there as we usually do, understand?'

Fintan stuffed the markers into his shirt. Yola took a deep breath. The men's eyes were on her. She touched St Christopher. 'Come on, Sailor – search.' Sailor did not move. He was lying on the path staring out into the minefield. Yola's mind whirled. Sailor never missed a search command! Was he sick? 'Search, boy,' she commanded. He whined but did not move. Oh God, I can't fail now, Yola thought.

Then Fintan said quietly, 'Perhaps he's found one.'

Yola stared. 'But … but it's only inches from the path!' She called Sailor back to her and then sent him out on his figure of eight loop. He passed the spot, looped back and sank to the ground. There was no doubt! There were murmurs of wonder from the men around. 'The bastards,' she said. 'Look, the ground is disturbed, I bet this is one of yours Fintan.'

Fintan dropped a marker on the spot while Yola, visibly shaken, played with Sailor on safe ground; Sailor was delighted with himself. And it was this more than anything that helped Yola fight back the scent of cinnamon that rose from her memory in choking clouds.

Then the work began. Left and right, left and right, Sailor looped, nose to the ground, tail wagging. The first steps onto the minefield were the worst. Like stepping into a pool with crocodiles. The men with her were professionals. As they advanced, the two men on the flanks advanced too, rolling out the tapes that would mark the edge of the checked ground. There! Sailor was down again! Fintan walked gingerly over and marked the spot, then Yola wrestled with the dog over his rubber bear, keeping him on safe ground the whole time. Soon the pattern of the minefield emerged. First three in a line, then a zigzag pattern. Then there was a long stretch with nothing except two markers on the old track.

'I bet those are anti-tank mines,' Yola said. They paused to give Sailor a rest. Fintan turned to look back.

'What are they doing back there?'

Yola followed his gaze. The parallel tapes were clearly visible. She could make out the zigzag line of markers, but beyond them were lights low to the ground. People seemed to be working there on hands and knees.

'They are digging the mines up, I think,' she said.

'But isn't that dangerous?'

'Yes,' she said, 'very, but most of these men are deminers or were soldiers once – they know what they are doing, I hope. Uncle Banda says that if the people can get back onto their land tonight, it can be done peaceably before anyone realises what's happening. They have a big stock of arms here, but the soldiers are away training across the river.'

She turned her back on the activity behind her and looked ahead. Fintan followed her gaze.

'Is no one defending the Noose lands, then? Surely we can't just walk in.'

'Yes, there are defenders,' Yola said. 'The boy I am seeking is one.'

'But ... I ... I thought he had been captured?'

'Yes, Fintan, he was. But it's his mind that is captive, not his body. We must be careful, he could be very dangerous.' Yola thought back to her mines awareness class and remembered with pain that nasty little look of triumph on Gabbin's face when he had scared poor Sister Martha. 'Let's go on, I think we are nearly there.'

◆　◇　◆

The washout – a steep-sided gully that had been cut into light-coloured gravels by the river in flood – appeared stark and bright across the track. On the opposite side it rose to a line of bushes.

'Get down both of you!' whispered Uncle Banda coming up behind them. 'Gabbin's post is just over there in those bushes. There are no mines now, but he won't hesitate to shoot. I just wonder why he hasn't challenged us yet.'

Yola felt a surge of anger. She had brought them through the minefield and she was damned if she were going to let Banda take over now.

'Perhaps he's dead!' she snapped. 'Anyway, I can't lie down.'

'But I'm going to call out to him! He will obey me.'

'No you are not! I want Gabbin back, I don't want a child soldier. Fintan, you hold Sailor. I'm giving the orders now so stay quiet and keep low.'

She hesitated at the gully edge, then she launched forward and down. Her artificial leg dug deep into the gravel and sent an avalanche of stones and pebbles bounding down the slope. It was at that moment, and too late, that she realised why she had not been challenged before. On top she had been a comfortable black on black, here she was black on white: the perfect target. She looked up towards the bushes above her. The metallic click of the rifle being cocked carried over the sound of the cascading stones. She could feel the rifle pointing at her like an invisible eye. She closed her eyes, waiting for the hammer blows of the bullets that would follow.

'*Stop!*' a boy's voice called in Kasembi. 'Don't move or I will shoot!'

Yola opened her eyes. She could see him. He had moved out from the shelter of the bushes and stood recklessly exposed against the moon-glow of the sky. She recognised the voice but it was twisted out of shape, somewhere between triumph and despair.

'I am Yola,' she called. 'Why do you stand in the open like a fool, Gabbin Abonda, where you can be shot!'

'You cannot shoot me. You are the fool. Your bullets will bounce off me. I have strong medicine.'

'What has given you this power, this medicine, mighty boy?'

'I have killed. I have this medicine because I have spilled the blood of my own kin.'

'Do you not recognise my voice, Gabbin Abonda?'

'Go away, I do not know you. I do not know myself. I have sold my soul by what I have done, all I can do is go on.' The boy's voice was rising. 'I can kill you ... nothing matters.'

Yola realised she was losing him. She'd never looked down the barrel of a rifle before. She must enter his world or perish.

'Mighty boy, there are those who still have power over you.'

'There are none!' he crowed.

What nonsense had he been fed? His voice was certain now, arrogant even, but she persisted.

'Those whose lives you have saved have power over you.'

'You are a *girl*, you have no power over me. I have saved no other life.'

Yola tingled – was there the tiniest hint of uncertainty when he said '... no other life?' She thrust for home.

'Yes, there is. There is another one here. It is your godfather, Banda.'

'He can't be, he is dead! I killed him!' Gabbin's voice was rising to a scream. Then, above her, Yola heard her uncle's voice boom out.

'Gabbin, I am your godfather. My name is Banda. I am the other whose life you saved. You aimed to miss me, you know that. Because of you, I live.'

Silence. Yola prayed that no one would move. Gabbin would need time to absorb this. But suddenly there was movement above her. Pebbles bounced and cascaded past. Banda was, even now, coming down the slope. She looked up: there he was, in stark relief against the white of the washout. This was folly. Yola knew how Gabbin's mind worked and she saw the movement as he swung his weapon to cover the new target.

'You are a ghost, Banda.' The voice was hysterical now. 'My bullets will pass through you. Look!'

'Look at the gravel, Gabbin,' Yola screamed, but her voice was shattered by a burst of gunfire. She could see the spurts of the striking bullets as they swept towards the figure above her. The muzzle flashes burned the corners of her eyes. She was next in the line of fire, but something heavy landed on top of her and swept and slid her down to the gully bottom; it was Fintan. The firing stopped. She looked up to where her uncle lay, a black crucifixion on the gravel slope. Irrational fury filled her; the boy had not let her finish her sentence.

'Look at the gravel, Gabbin, no ghost would leave footprints like these!' she shouted.

The gouged prints stood out, shadowed in the moonlight. Sand trickled from them. Yola moved to sit and an arm closed about her from behind. The silence stretched and stretched.

'Don't move, he's coming!' Fintan whispered.

The boy appeared, side-stepping down the slope, his gun at the ready. He reached the bottom and looked up. They heard a whimper. The barrel was dipping. He was looking at the cruciform figure above him. It stirred.

'Banda?' he called.

'Are you going to shoot me, Gabbin?'

'Oh Banda!' gasped the boy. His rifle fell from his hands. 'Oh Banda!' He was scrambling up the slope. As he climbed they could see the man turn to sit. He reached down to the climbing boy and pulled him to him. Gabbin fell on him, touching, feeling and eventually believing that he was real.

Yola sat looking up at them and relief flooded into her. She leant back against Fintan, who was holding her from behind, his arms locked, his chin resting on her head.

'So this is Gabbin, your fiancé, the six-foot warrior with a spear?'

'It was only his spear that was six-foot long! And he's my cousin, we could never have married.'

Once again her memory conjured up a smell – not cinnamon this time, but mint. She was back in the clinic in Dublin. Catherine was squeezing toothpaste on to her brush and Yola was telling her about Gabbin's proposal. 'She'll tell him, you know,' Brigid had said. She'd forgotten, she couldn't believe it. All this time, Fintan had thought she was engaged. She started to chuckle. Then she decided to postpone it. She'd take Fintan to see Shimima and Kimba – that would be the time for laughing. She leant back.

'Fintan,' she said, 'I'd like you to go on holding me like this.'

'For how long?' asked Fintan gently.

'Forever?'

'No problem.'

But it was.

24

Before the Dawn can Come

A whistle shrilled in the distance; the four figures in the washout froze. The other boys! Of course, they would have heard the shots. Yola could see Banda and Gabbin talking, then Gabbin put his fingers in his mouth and a piercing whistle rang out through the gully. Fintan's grip on Yola tightened. There was a clatter above them, but it was just Sailor surfing down to them on a small crest of gravel; he must have thought that Fintan had whistled to him. Yola hugged him and he settled down between her knees. She wondered at her sensations. Perhaps it was exhaustion, perhaps euphoria, but her mind was electric, moving so fast that everything else about her seemed slowed down. When Gabbin skidded down the slope, picked up his rifle and scrambled up through the sand towards his observation post, it was an urgent scrabble, but what Yola saw was every graceful move of his young body. Uncle Banda came down to tell them what was happening, and Yola knew what he was going to say before he said it.

'It is dangerous for me to appear until the boys are prepared. Gabbin will explain to them that I am not a ghost, that they must look at the sand and see my footprints. He says that things have been very bad since I left, so the boys are jumpy and trigger-happy.' He climbed back out of the gully, the way they had come in.

Yola was reluctant to move, but they were very conspicuous where they sat on the gully floor. Fintan helped her to her feet and they struggled up the slope on Gabbin's side. They found Gabbin's out-post shelter and watched from its shadow.

The boys began to arrive, wary silhouettes against the white gravel. Yola, her awareness still tuned to the highest pitch, saw aggression, incredulity and fear in their approaches, and, to her immense surprise, a girl.

Gabbin talked to them in Kasembi. Yola had to smile, recognising in the young boy Father's formal manner of speech.

'Comrades, a great joy has come to me and my joy will be yours if you see me. Do you see me?'

'We see you.' The reply was wary.

'Do you hear me?' Gabbin was determined.

'We hear you.'

He talked of their grief when he had been made to shoot at the instructor that had been good to them, his own godfather, Banda. But he now had news ... good news ...

'What's he saying?' whispered Fintan. 'It takes so long.'

'Shh, this is Africa, Fintan, certain things must be done slowly. She took his hand. After a while she said, 'Look, look, they are putting down their guns.'

'Captain Banda,' Gabbin called, 'we see you'.

There was a pause, then Uncle Banda's voice boomed out across the gully. 'I see you boys. I see you! I have come.' One of the smaller boys turned to run, but another grabbed and held him. Banda stepped warily down onto the gravel. 'Do not shoot me boys, I am no ghost. Watch how my feet break the gravel.' Yola heard the small gasp as his feet dug firmly into the soft surface. Then Uncle Banda chuckled, 'Come boys, have you lost your tongues?'

'Captain Banda, we see you?' The response was ragged at first. Then all together in obvious joy, 'Banda, we see you!' Yola thought they were going to run to him, but their discipline was too good. She watched, fascinated, as a thousand microscopic moments – disbelief, wonder, joy, relief – flickered through the group. She heard their combined whispered 'Waaah' when Banda struggled up and stood in front of them and she realised, at that moment, that they loved him.

He called them into a semicircle about him and told them that the minefield had been penetrated and that soon the government troops would arrive. He thanked them for saving his life by tying his legs loosely, and he thanked Gabbin for shooting wide. But he said that being thrown to the crocodiles by his own comrades had made him understand the stupidity of fighting. Tonight they had one more mission under his command, and that was to help him capture their evil instructors and to destroy the ammunition dump in the Noose, because once that was gone, the soldiers would go too.

'There is to be no more fighting. The Noose lands do not belong to Kasemba or to Murabende or to the KLA. They belong to the farmers who are waiting, with their cattle, to come back in. You will not be punished. I have made arrangements for you stay with families who will look after you. I will still be your leader, but now it will be to help you to go to school, perhaps even to find jobs. I have spoken!'

Yola realised it was time for her to move. Holding Fintan with one hand and Sailor with the other, she walked out onto the little rise above the gathering. The drama of the moment appealed to her – a ghost returned, a black girl with a stiff leg, a white boy and a black-and-white dog sitting to her command –

but not one of the kids stirred. Eyes moved perhaps, but they would not turn until Captain Banda released them. She watched them individually and wondered what histories they had and what futures were in store for them. Then she realised they were all looking at her and Fintan because Uncle Banda was talking about them. There was a soft 'Waaah!' of appreciation.

◆ ◇ ◆

As Uncle Banda issued instructions, Yola remembered her aerial view of the Noose from the aeroplane. She saw again the threads of smoke, the tracks, even the landing stage where she now guessed the troops from Murabende landed. Then Gabbin was talking; there were boys in outposts to be called in. He seemed to be particularly worried about one boy, Ukebu, who was watching at the landing stage.

'What about the instructors, Uncle Banda, why haven't they come?' Yola asked. 'They must have heard Gabbin's shots. What sort of men are they?'

'They are Kasemban rebels, the one to watch out for is the tallest, he is called Juvimba. It is as I had guessed, they have been drinking hard. The boys will deal with them.'

Yola had been looking at the boys, guessing that there were potential killers among them. She raised her voice. 'Boys!' she called. 'You will take no guns!' There was a stunned silence.

'Yola, you'll never! They are trained ...' Banda was worried.

'Boys, and the secret girl among you,' she said smiling, 'you have won freedom tonight. Free people do not need guns. I have walked through your minefield with a friend, a dog and just one leg. There are other ways of doing things. I want these men captured but not hurt. No guns.'

The pause seemed to last for minutes, in fact it was just seconds. A figure moved and came forward – tattered combats, a baggy shirt – and laid its rifle at Yola's feet. Then it looked up at Yola with bright, clear eyes. Yes, she was a girl!

The pile of guns grew. As each one came, Yola felt them searching her face as if to understand her. Gabbin was talking and she realised how good he must have been as a soldier. He knew where everyone was and who should be sent to bring them in. He issued orders but they didn't seem to be orders, so even older boys obeyed. He was lucky, she thought, he had a real home to go to, but what about the others? Fintan was getting restless and asked Uncle Banda to translate while he talked to Gabbin about the missing mines. In a little time, Gabbin called another boy over. The four of them had their heads together. She saw Fintan hold up three fingers; surely that meant three mines. She calculated: of the six mines left in Murabende, two had exploded, injuring the government deminers. If the boys knew of three that meant that there was one mine left unaccounted for. She thought of Hans: 'Until the last one is found our work is crippled!' Fintan would not stop till he found that mine. A chill – a premonition, perhaps – ran down her back like the first shiver of a coming fever. The night's work was not over.

They arrived at the training camp; the boys had gone ahead and had done their work efficiently, and without guns. Three men were leaning against the wall, trussed up like chickens. Two on each side sagged drunkenly, but the one in the middle was staring at her. Uncle Banda sent a boy running down the path towards the jetty to tell Ukebu and to warn them if the rebel troops landed. A ghetto blaster roared out from inside a hut. Yola asked one of the boys to turn it off. She wanted to see what these instructors were like. As she approached, the one in the middle worked his mouth and then spat at her, his gob rolling in the dust.

'Yola Abonda,' he said.

Could he know her? She was startled; she'd never seen him before.

'Oh yes, I know you, and I know your rich family. May you, like your ancestors before you, rot!' He was tall, and he twisted against the cords binding him. 'You are going to let them kill us, aren't you? You've taken their guns so they can do it by hand – we've taught them that too!' He laughed. 'Go on flinch, bitch! But you are a thief, and your father's a thief!'

Suddenly he sagged, and Yola guessed he was still drunk. When he went on it was in low, bitter voice, almost a whisper.

'You owe me a favour, daughter of Abonda. Your family stole someone from me. I want you take her a message.'

At last images began to click into focus in Yola's mind: Sindu pleading 'But Juvimba?' and a man's broken watch spilled on the floor. Feelings of revulsion and guilt rose up in her. She wanted to walk away, but she couldn't.

'Yes, Juvimba. I will give Sindu your message.' Then she added with sudden inspiration, 'And you will give me a piece of information that I need.'

'Why should I?' he sneered.

'Because I could tell Sindu about your cruelty to the children here and the evil things you have done. She's lazy, but she likes children for all that. She would not love you for what you have done here. Give me your message. Then, if you answer my question, I will see no need to tell her the truth about you.'

Yola listened like a priest at confession – bewildered – trying to reconcile words of love with knowing that this was the man who had ordered Gabbin to shoot his own godfather. When he'd finished, she asked her question. She doubted that she would get a useful answer, but she tried.

'Now my question to you. You received six special land-mines from Murabende. We know where all but one of these are. Where is the remaining mine?' She watched his bloodshot eyes flicking, looking for escape, but there was none.

'It is here, but you won't get it.'

'Why?'

'Because it is in the weapon store over there.' He raised his chin towards a low building on the opposite side of the clearing. 'But you will never open it. It is behind thirty centimetres of reinforced concrete and a two-inch thick steel door.'

'Where's the key?'

'In Murabende, with the white commander.'

'When are they due back?'

'Now!'

Juvimba had achieved his aim. Yola gave up. Her sound leg was tired beyond belief; her stump felt raw. They couldn't get into the ammunition store and the KLA troops were coming. Thanks to her, they hadn't even a rifle to stop them. There was a folding chair outside the tent, she flopped into it and put her head in her hands. All the KLA had to do was open the store and they would have enough guns to drive them, and everyone else, back out of the Noose. She'd even cleared a road through the mines for them – they could be in Nopani by daybreak! She'd probably started a war, not stopped one. She became aware of Fintan squatting beside her, stroking her shoulders, asking her questions, but what was the point.

'You were asking him about the missing mine, weren't you? Does he know?' he asked. 'The boys know where the other three are, that leaves one, *just one*! We've got to find it.'

Yola buried her face deeper. She needed to think; they should be trying to get out of here, not talking mines. But he was pressing her. 'Where is it, Yola?' She had seen this obstinate streak in his father. She started to cry, but then knew it was no use.

'It's in the weapon store, over there, look, where Uncle Banda's going. But Fintan, it is reinforced concrete and he says the door is steel.'

If Yola had had any control over Fintan before, she had none now. He was possessed. It was as if the guilt and shame that had built up over his father's involvement in the mines were erupting uncontrollably inside him. Yola straightened up. Her sharpened perception returned and she felt she was watching the whole scene from a great height but with absolute clarity.

At Fintan's orders, Gabbin cleared the child soldiers away from the area of the ammunition store. Her mind centred on a point, in the centre of which was the steel door, on this her whole being was focussed. Fintan and Uncle Banda were labouring in turn. They had found a sledge-hammer and were hammering, first at the lock, then at the hinges, anywhere to find a point of weakness. The hammer blows fell silently, a fraction of a second later the clang arrived, and Yola was back in class in Ireland listening to the teacher explaining what a laggard sound was compared to light. She saw Fintan peel off his shirt; his white torso gleamed in the pale light. She looked anxiously at the moon, it was dipping towards the trees again. How long had they? Where were the rebel soldiers?

✦ ✧ ✦

Fintan stood in front of her. The sweat ran off him in rivers. Uncle Banda glistened, his chest was heaving.

'There's no way. We can't do it,' Fintan said. 'They've welded chunks of metal around the lock and hinges. We can't get a swipe at anything. Damn and blast them!' He threw his sodden shirt on the ground. 'Where are those soldiers? We'd better go.'

'A boy has gone down to the jetty. He will give us warning,' said Uncle Banda, squatting down, head between his knees. Juvimba's voice cut in abrasively.

'Stay here. Ask them for the key. Even better, why don't you take a mine detector to it and blow the bloody lot of you up in the process.'

Both Fintan and Yola froze for a moment ... of course. The mine was programmed to explode on hearing a mine detector – but they didn't have one, there wasn't one within miles. Anyway, the sound would be too weak to penetrate the concrete of the bunker.

'Come on,' Yola said, 'we must get the boys out of here before the soldiers come ... Fintan?'

But Fintan wasn't listening. 'My shirt?' he muttered. Yola was holding out her hand for a lift out of the chair. *'Where is my shirt!'* Yola was shocked, he'd never ever raised his voice before, least of all at her. Gabbin picked up the shirt and handed it to him; it hung like something dead. 'Gabbin, quick, quick, ghetto blaster, radio, you know ... in the hut ... quick!' Uncle Banda translated, but Gabbin had already gone. Fintan was searching frantically through the pockets in his shirt. 'Got it,' he muttered and pulled a tape cassette from his pocket. *'Clear the area!'* he yelled. 'Where's Gabbin?' But Gabbin was there, holding a huge two-speaker recorder. Fintan was fumbling to get the cassette out of its box. At last, Yola realised what he was at. This was the special programme tape containing the recorded sounds of all the different mine detectors – he'd put it in his pocket after talking to Hans!

'No!' yelled Yola. You can't! You won't have time to get away.'

She lunged for the tape but he snatched it out of reach. Holding the tape in his mouth, he flicked out the music tape that was in the drive, thrust the special tape into the machine and pressed the button.

'One … two … thr–' he counted and the recorded shriek of a mine detector rang out. 'Jeez, that's short. I can run fast, but not that fast.'

'You can't, you can't, oh don't,' pleaded Yola, but Fintan was tilting the ghetto blaster to get the light on the buttons.

'Got it! I think we can. It depends on what's on the other side of this tape. When Fintan pressed the play button the camp area was filled with wild Irish music. Yola wondered where she was; she thought of the dancing lab technician. Then Fintan was beside her, explaining, reassuring her.

'See what I'll do, there's no panic. I'll rewind a couple of minutes of the music, then, while the music is playing out, I'll walk quietly back – I won't even run. When the music finishes, the tape will reverse, only then will it play the mine detector noises. If we're lucky we'll hear a pop as the mine goes off. Get everyone ready to go and we'll be out of here in ten minutes.'

Yola tried to get out of the low chair, but couldn't. She heard the falsetto twitter as Fintan rewound a generous few minutes' worth of tape. Then he was gone.

Uncle Banda called the boys and got them to untie the feet of the two drunken instructors so that they could walk, but told them to leave Juvimba to him. Fintan reached the door of the ammunition dump; they all turned to watch. He waved – a warning, perhaps – and bent to the ghetto blaster. Even from a distance the volume of the music was impressive. Then, calmly, Fintan began walking towards them.

Only Juvimba saw the boy soldier who had suddenly appeared in the clearing, noticed that he had a gun and knew that this was Ukebu, one of his own – a little killer. Juvimba's mind worked fast: Ukebu had obviously dealt with the scout Uncle

Banda had sent down to bring him back. All this meant just one thing – fortune had turned in Juvimba's favour and the KLA troops had landed without the alarm being raised. He filled his lungs and yelled.

'Shoot him, Ukebu! Shoot the white man. I am Captain Juvimba. *Shoot him!*'

The boy's rifle jerked up as if pulled by a string; Fintan saw him. Perhaps the boy was confused by the music, perhaps he didn't recognise Juvimba's voice, but the split-second delay was vital. There was a log beside the path. Fintan hurled himself over it. The boy's rifle rattled out, bullets kicking up dust along the length of the log. Like startled rabbits, everyone who could dived for cover. Only Yola and Juvimba remained in the open. Yola sat frozen in her chair. She heard a scuffle behind her, but dared not move. Perhaps the boy wouldn't see her. He was looking about him, trying to locate Juvimba. But he kept his gun pointed at the log. The music was rising. Surely this was the climax? In a minute the tape would reverse and Fintan was pinned down only metres from the steel doors. She heard Juvimba's voice low beside her.

'I don't need a messenger now, do I?' Then he raised his voice. 'Shoot the girl here beside me.' Then he changed his mind. 'No! Turn the music off first. They have no guns.' For one fateful second the boy hesitated.

It was a burst of three shots and it came from behind Yola. The muzzle flashes lit up the ground around her. She flinched and then looked at the boy in amazement. He lurched – surely he'd been hit! He was staring at his hands; his menacing profile had changed. His gun was gone, blown out of his hands by that single burst of fire. The music stopped. Everything stopped. Everybody seemed to have lost the power to move. Seconds ticked by. The tape would be reversing.

Fintan burst from behind the log and hurtled towards her, foreshortened in her view, like a sprinter from the blocks. But he had waited too long. The familiar screech of a mine detector, magnified a hundred times by the ghetto blaster, screamed out.

It was the steel door that blew first, arching lazily above Fintan's head like a piece of bent cardboard. Then the concrete top lifted skywards, broken into great gobbets of concrete held together by steel rods; still no sound had reached her. All colour was gone save for one intense centre of red and orange. She saw the blast hit Fintan, throw him up and forward like someone caught by a wave. The boy soldier, Ukebu, was spinning like a top. Uncle Banda wrenched her to the ground as something hard crashed into the side of the hut.

Letting in the Light

It was an hour before Fintan was recovered enough to be moved. The boys found a stretcher and put him on to it, ready for a rapid exit. Uncle Banda went down to the jetty to investigate.

'The KLA have gone,' he said. 'They probably thought the government army was here with that explosion. Anyway, there is nothing now for them to attack with.'

Fintan was holding Yola's hand. She wanted to stay with him, but there was something she felt she had to do first. Juvimba was dead: the piece of concrete that had struck the hut had killed him outright. She couldn't look at him, but she asked the boys to take the ropes off his feet and hands – she felt she owed this to Sindu. Perhaps his role in all this need never be known. The boys joked as they worked and Yola shuddered.

Suddenly, Yola was conscious of a presence beside her. It was the girl-boy, her friend of the clear eyes.

Uncle Banda nodded and said in English, 'We call him Jimmy.' Yola wondered if she saw a wink. Then he switched to Kasembi. 'It was Jimmy who fired the shot that saved us. He knew where Juvimba's rifle was in the hut and dived for it. That was a very fine shot – to hit the rifle and not hurt your friend.' The child's face lit up; she looked changed when she smiled.

'Oh I don't mind if I kill him, we all hates Ukebu. I aim for his rifle. He has even stronger medicine than Gabbin, see. Captain Juvimba make him kill his own brother. I couldn't kill him. Bullets would bounce off him with no harm.'

Later, Yola was proud of the fact that she hadn't said anything to 'Jimmy' that night, apart from thanking her. But if Juvimba had been alive she would have broken him into bits. Could a girl like this, or indeed any of the others, ever be normal again?

With first light the people of the Noose began to pour in along the cleared corridor through the minefield. The first one or two came walking lightly, nervously, expecting to step on a mine at any moment, but soon the trickle became a flow. Women came, struggling up the gully side with huge bundles on their heads. Jostling cattle came through, their drovers anxiously beating them away from the tapes that the deminers had raised on stakes beside the gap.

Fintan was able to walk again, limping, but otherwise sound as they walked out against the throng of people. Yola felt that it should be a triumphant march with cheering and clapping and grateful handshakes, but it wasn't. The people streaming in spared hardly a glance for them; their eyes were set on homes they hadn't seen for years. At one point there was rough shouting ahead and everyone pulled in to the sides as a column of government soldiers came through at a run. The army captain barked at them to get out of the way. Yola shouted at him that there was no one left to fight, but he didn't hear or turn.

They walked out three by three. Uncle Banda, Yola and the girl-boy with the bright eyes and murderous ways were behind. The other trio walked in front: Sailor, on his lead, then Fintan and Gabbin, holding hands, as Africans like to do.

Yola looked at them with a sigh and said to herself, 'My boys.'

EPILOGUE

Cutting the Noose

A flush of green now blankets the hill where Managu, the bull, wandered while Gabbin played in the Russian tank. The deminers have stripped the hill bare of bush in their search for landmines. The larger trees remain, as do the paths, persisting as paths do, even when everything around them changes. Hans looked at his watch.

'You have half an hour if Fintan is to get his flight to Simbada,' he said, and climbed into the driver's seat.

It was Shimima who had sent them. 'Yola, my little friend, there are ghosts still on the hill where you went that day. They will come back to haunt you if you do not go. Go with your friend and take Gabbin with you, too; it is important that he goes.'

But Gabbin would not come. He sat in the back of the Land-cruiser beside Uncle Banda and looked away from the hill. Often since they had returned from the Noose, he had dark moods and would be silent or say bitter things that reminded Yola of the time he had fooled poor Sister Martha. Yola had lost Gabbin; he was Uncle Banda's now and she missed him with an empty pain. She sighed and took Fintan's hand. They could walk side by side now because people no longer feared to walk at the edges of the path. It was all so changed. The bushes she had had to jump to see over were gone. They could see right over the town.

Fintan was going home. She had been overjoyed when Father had told her that the people of the Noose had contributed to her fare so that she could go back to school in Ireland. But what would Fintan feel about her then, a lame little school-girl in an Irish convent?

They turned a bend, and there it was: the cinnamon tree. The branch curved down, inviting her to jump again. Managu's bell was surely tolling on the hillside below. In a second she'd be whole again. It had never happened! Then the ghosts were around her, plucking at her, mocking her. The ugly scar seared into the bark of the tree glared at her. Suddenly the smell of cinnamon was welling up, swirling inside her head. Gabbin was calling 'Yola ... Yola ... I'm coming!' But she had been unconscious when he had come to save her life that time beneath the tree. Why must the spirits mock her? Then she realised that someone was shaking her. She looked up; Fintan's face swam in her rising tears.

'Yola, listen to me, listen ... he's coming!'

'Who ... who?'

'Why Gabbin, of course!'

At once Yola was alert, listening with her whole body. She took a deep breath and the air was clean and fresh, blowing the cinnamon scent from her mind. Fintan stepped back.

'I won't be far,' he whispered. He bent and kissed her, a light, rich kiss that seemed to be an echo of everything she felt for him. Her mind filled with music, as if all the discord and dissonance of the past years were resolving itself now into one mighty chord. She could hear the pat of running feet on the path, and Gabbin called.

'Yola, I'm here!'

ABOUT THE CINNAMON TREE

There is a cinnamon tree, and there was a landmine under it. I could see the rim of it sticking out through the red earth before Vincent, an Angolan deminer, sent me away so that he could lift it and make it safe.

In 1998 I travelled to Angola, inspired by Princess Diana, who had chosen to wake the world to the evil of landmines by visiting this, the landmines capital of the world. I wanted to write this book, but first I needed to meet the victims and to see how landmines were located and dealt with. Angola has been at war for thirty-eight years: first a war of independence from Portugal, and then twenty-four years of civil war. During this time, ten million landmines have been laid there, most of which are still in the ground. Over 70,000 people have lost limbs and many, particularly children, have died.

But Kasemba, my imaginary country, is not Angola. You will not find it on a map of Africa, nor will you find a Yola or a Gabbin quite as I describe them. Nevertheless, much of what I have told in *The Cinnamon Tree* is real.

There are a number of demining groups in Angola, but I was looked after by a wonderful organisation called Norwegian People's Aid. In *The Cinnamon Tree*, when Yola travels from Nopani to Simbada, I am describing a trip very like my own from Luanda, the capital of Angola, to Lobito, where Norwegian People's Aid have their field-station. It was there that I saw dogs being trained to sniff out mines. I watched a beautiful German Shepherd looping left and right, just as Sailor did for Yola on her nighttime expedition, his tail waving with excitement. Then he sank to the ground, his Angolan handler marked the spot and a supervisor came with a spade and carefully dug up a large anti-tank mine. Incidentally, Yola's nighttime expedition was far more dangerous than she realised. Responsible deminers would not walk into a minefield like that.

Later, I was taken to the little town of Gabela, where I saw a real mine-clearance in operation. There was a hill, and a Russian tank – just like the one Gabbin was playing in when he lost Managu the bull – but there were no boys near the tank while I was there. Discipline was tight. The Angolan deminers worked in pairs, each pair fifty metres apart, in case of accidents. Only a week before, a deminer had been injured when he accidentally pulled a tripwire attached to a hand grenade in the bushes. Vincent, the supervisor, showed me a stake marking the place where they had recently found a landmine. Beside the spot was a bent stick with a piece of string attached. It was a bird trap, set by some youngster while the mine was still in the ground. When he knelt to set his trap, he was only centimetres away from the mine. Later that day, Vincent called me over to look at a mine they had uncovered under a tree. He pointed out how it had been placed there so that anyone trying to climb the tree would step on it, a soldier or a sniper perhaps – or even a girl like Yola. Vincent took his knife out and broke off a piece of the bark, smiling as he asked me to smell it. Yes, the smell was cinnamon.

For Yola's family life I turned to the people that I had lived among once for a year, on the shores of Lake Victoria in Kenya. Here important men, like Yola's father, often had several wives. By giving a good bride-price for a new young bride, the wealthy man could help a neighbour and, at the same time, get welcome help for his senior wife. Often this worked well, even for the young bride. She moved from being a drudge at home, perhaps, to being the wife of an important man, with both status and security. If there were problems it was the senior wife who kept the peace. In Africa, age and wisdom are respected. Any man of importance is expected to show wisdom and good judgement. Father, with his almost telepathic understanding of people, is a portrait of a wise Kenyan I knew.

How is it then that wise and gentle people find themselves locked in war? One of the reasons is that unscrupulous people make money out of selling arms. In *The Cinnamon Tree,* Mr Birthistle represents the underbelly of the arms trade – people who sell guns and ammunition to anyone who is prepared to pay for them. But arms dealers are not the only offenders. Both governments and arms manufacturers make the money to develop their Star Wars weapons by selling armaments. We are disgusted at the thought of germ warfare, but rifles, like germs, spread the disease of war.

Some guns are now so light that children can handle them. Gabbin, at age eleven, could easily strip, clean and fire a Kalashnikov rifle. It looks like a toy, and weighs only 4.3 kilos, but yet it is capable of firing 600 bullets a minute. Every day, children are taken from their families and taught to fight. There is nothing romantic about this. Children are often given a choice: kill your own parents or be killed yourself. If they do this, they are so torn by guilt and grief that they can be made to believe or do anything. Crazed children, persuaded that they are invincible, are forced to lead attacks or to walk through minefields.

The Cinnamon Tree was written for you to enjoy. If, however, you would like to do something for one or other of the issues in this book, the following organisations should give you a start:

1. Support the *International Campaign to Ban Landmines*. You will find their website at http://www.icbl.org. You will find *Norwegian People's Aid* at http://www.npaid.org

2. Raise money for demining. In Ireland, donations can be sent to the *Irish Red Cross Society*, 'Landmine Appeal', 16 Merrion Square, Dublin 2.

3. Campaign against child soldiers. *Rädda Barnen* (Sweden's Save the Children) produce an excellent newsletter in English, *Children of War*, available at http://www.rb.se

4. Campaign against the arms trade. In Ireland, *Afri* are active in trying to keep the arms business out of Ireland. Write to Afri at Grand Canal House, Lower Rathmines Road, Dublin 6.

5. In Britain, the *Campaign Against the Arms Trade* (CAAT) have an informative website at http://www.caat.demon.co.uk and publish a comprehensive newsletter.